OCT 1 3 2000

GLENALLYN'S BRIDE

Queen Johanna destroyed the House of Frazer at Dundallon, after the murder of James I. Innes Frazer, step-sister to Sir Archibald, escaped but was captured by a band of beggars. The leader of the beggars, Ruari Stewart, offers her as a bride to Glenallyn. Innes refuses, only to become a servant of the Queen at Edinburgh Castle, where she again meets James Livingstone who was responsible for slaughtering the Frazers. Innes knows that she must find Ruari Stewart, and one day she might become Glenallyn's bride.

MARY CUMMINS

GLENALLYN'S BRIDE

Complete and Unabridged

LINFORD
Leicester

First published in Great Britain in 1981

First Linford Edition
published 2006

British Library CIP Data

Cummins,Mary
  Glenallyn's bride.—Large print ed.—
Linford romance library
1. Love stories
2. Large type books
I. Title
823.9'14 [F]

ISBN 1–84617–263–2

Published by
F. A. Thorpe (Publishing)
Anstey, Leicestershire

Set by Words & Graphics Ltd.
Anstey, Leicestershire
Printed and bound in Great Britain by
T. J. International Ltd., Padstow, Cornwall

This book is printed on acid-free paper

1

For the past week a strange quietness had hung over Dundallon. The old tower house, built over a hundred years before in 1328, was a fine strong building surrounded on three sides by a curtain wall, but although a huge log fire smouldered in the great hall, there was not enough heat to keep out the chill of a day in late February.

On the ground floor some of the store rooms lay almost empty because Sir Archibald Frazer had ensured that his men were well provided with equipment when he had ridden out a few days before to join the King's court at Blackfriars monastery in Perth. He had left his wife, Lady Eleanor, in charge of Dundallon; which included a fair quantity of remaining supplies, a number of men and maidservants, a few horses, his young step-sister Innes

1

and his two small children, Robert and Isobel.

Both Eleanor and Innes had sulked at Archibald's departure because he had promised to take them to court at the next opportunity; and the two young women had spent long, happy hours helping to design court dresses which would not make a laughing stock of the Frazers when the Queen and her ladies set eyes on them.

Eleanor had not been to court for some months and Archibald had considered that his step-sister was far too young for such frivolities. Recently Innes had passed the age of seventeen and Eleanor had insisted that she be given her place amongst the other ladies who congregated round the Royal couple. King James the First of Scotland was a fine, handsome man with a loving and devoted wife, Queen Johanna, and there were always personable young men at court. Eleanor noted the signs which indicated that Mistress Innes was fast growing up, and in need of a husband.

Archibald's father had married Lady Jane Innes when he was in his middle years and she a young bride no older than his only son. Lady Jane had died in childbirth and Sir Hector Frazer of Dundallon had ridden off to fight the English for his King. He had not cared whether he lived or died, and soon Archibald had fallen heir to the estate and to rearing his baby step-sister. He had left her to the rough but loving care of Janet Balfour, her nurse, and when he married his Eleanor, she had found the girl in great need of tuition in the finer skills of a woman's life. Innes knew how to read and write, and had ridden out on a wolf hunt with some of Archibald's men to keep an eye on her; but she had to be taught how to sew the fine silks and velvets she was entitled to wear as befitted her station in life, even though she would never make a needlewoman.

It had taken Lady Eleanor a few

months to encourage Innes into desiring fine clothes and a visit to Court. She had been cross with Archibald when he refused to consider taking his ladies, even though her figure was now trim again after birthing their second child, the baby Isobel.

'Why don't you take us, Archibald?' she had pleaded, and had been surprised by the fury and impatience of his answer. Normally he was an even-tempered man and devoted to her. They had married for love, even as the King had married for love, and Eleanor had been deeply hurt by the set-down which Archibald delivered. He would not be gone for more than a week, he promised, but now the week was up and a few more days besides, and the old castle seemed to be suspended in time until the master rode home again.

Innes found her sister-in-law out of temper with her and ready to find fault when Eleanor forgot she was now past seventeen, and clattered down to the kitchens to beg a honeycake from

Mirren Cameron, who could bake pastries as light as air. The kitchen was new since Lady Eleanor came to Dundallon and it had a huge fireplace and three windows. There was a stone sink and a drain which carried the sewage away so that it did not contaminate the well in the courtyard.

There was also a new guardrobe constructed near the private apartments and this, too, had been built to discharge its contents down the wall of the east wing and into the restless surge of the North Sea which afforded protection against attack. Five years before, King James had granted a licence to crenellate, and Archibald had been satisfied that Dundallon was as well protected as any tower-house in the land. He was by nature a peaceful man, but in recent months he had been in the company of Sir Robert Graham too much for Lady Eleanor's liking, and Sir Robert had made no secret of the fact that he was at loggerheads with the King.

'Why, the man talks treason,' Eleanor had whispered to Archibald after they had entertained Sir Robert and his men one cold November evening.

'He has his reasons,' Archibald growled. 'The King is a tyrant when he pleases and takes land where he will. Graham's nephew is his latest victim and who knows where his eyes will fall next? Would you be so pleased with the King if Dundallon were taken?'

Eleanor's lips tightened. Her father was an Ogilvy and a King's man. He had said that James was the finest King to govern Scotland for decades and that just such a man was needed to keep the more powerful barons under control. He doled out harsh justice but he was rarely unfair. Perhaps Archibald had not been told what Graham's nephew had done to lose his lands!

But Archibald had not been in the mood to argue and when Innes had been pert to him because of her disappointment, he had ordered her to stay in her room with the barest necessities for two days. She had been chilled to the bone, and old Janet Balfour, who had shared her punishment, had snivelled with cold ever since.

'The fires are low,' Innes complained to Eleanor.

'We need the men home for log gathering,' her sister-in-law said, briefly. 'They will not be feeling the cold at Blackfriars. The King plays tennis and other games. The men will have plenty of exercise and I dare say the Queen and her ladies will exercise their tongues.'

'I hate Archibald,' Innes pouted sullenly, and Eleanor rounded on her.

'That is enough, Mistress Innes,' she cried, her eyes flashing. 'You can go to your room until you learn better manners. I have had enough of you.'

'But I was going to see the babes!' Innes protested.

'They will survive without your attention,' said Eleanor.

She knew she was being impatient

with Innes, who often said things she did not mean; but she had experienced a strange cold sick feeling in her heart, and the quiet of Dundallon had been full of foreboding rather than peace. There would be no lightness of spirit until Archibald rode home again. Eleanor did not trust Sir Robert Graham and could have wished a better friend for her husband.

Janet Balfour grumbled noisily as Innes slowly made her way to their bedchamber. It grew dark early and they were only allowed one candle. Mistress Innes was a spoilt young woman and needed a good man to keep her in order. Janet had married young and now her daughter was married to a farmer who dug his plot on the north side of the estate, and brought up a brood of children on what he could wrench from the soil. Janet managed a basket or two of extras from the kitchens, especially during festivities such as All Hallows Eve or after a wolf hunt.

Suddenly a cry went up from somewhere in the castle and Innes' heart leapt. Archibald was home! She began to clatter towards the stone stairs which would take her down to the great hall, but Janet stayed her hand.

'Not yet, Mistress!' she urged. 'Let the lady greet the master herself. There will be time enough for you. Do ye wish to gain her displeasure on both of us again?'

Innes hesitated. Eleanor had been tetchy since her baby was born. Perhaps it was best to be circumspect.

'The peephole!' she said to Janet. 'Come on and we'll look through the peephole.'

'No' me, Mistress,' said Janet. 'I'll light the candle and stir up the fire a wee. Come along to bed when you have looked down on the master. He'll send for you soon enough if he has brought a present from his travels.'

Innes had discovered the peephole one day when she was a child playing along the corridor above the great hall.

9

She was slender enough to wriggle into a small aperture and there she could look down on to the great hall and see the guests who had gathered there to greet Archibald and Eleanor. Usually it was another baron and his men, being afforded food and shelter, but sometimes their ladies would be with them, since Archibald was known as a gracious host. Few people travelled abroad other than in a sizeable party because of the beggars who roamed the countryside. The King had passed a law requiring all beggars to be licensed, but the law was not always upheld.

Now, as Innes ran to her peephole, she looked down on a scene of confusion. Archibald had not yet arrived but Will Cowan, Mirren's son, was lying in front of the fire in the great hall whilst Lady Eleanor knelt beside him and servants rushed to do her bidding. Will was filthy with mud and there was a gash on his cheek, oozing blood.

'Ye must hide, my lady,' he was

crying. 'It's all gone wrong. The King . . . the King has been murdered . . . murdered . . . '

'Oh God,' Eleanor whispered. 'I knew it. In my heart I knew it.'

'They are at my heels. Tell them it's no' Sir Archibald . . . it's . . . it's . . . '

Innes could hear no more and even as she watched Mirren gave a great cry and cradled Will's head in her arms. But already they could hear the shouts of men and the clatter of horses as they rode into the courtyard, and the great hall seemed to be full of men and women as the servants scurried in from the kitchens, their eyes wide with terror as they looked to Lady Eleanor for guidance and protection. Doors had been barred but were soon broken down as a party of men, bestial in their ferocity, burst into the great hall. Their leader, a bull-necked man with scarlet face and thick heavy limbs, had grabbed Lady Eleanor so that Innes almost cried out in her fear. The man was shouting that Sir Archibald had turned traitor and had aided Graham in murdering the King, and the Queen had ordered the destruction of every man concerned, even to the families of those directly implicated.

Innes never knew how long she remained inside her peephole. Half-fainting and with eyes full of horror, she watched the Lady Eleanor and the maidservants being ravished before they were put to the sword, and listened to the raucous commands of the leader. Servants and henchmen who had been hiding were put to the sword and Innes cowered in her hiding place as heavy-booted feet pounded the corridor and doors were thrown open. She heard Janet Balfour's scream of terror, then there was silence from the direction of her own room, and further along the corridors her small nephew and baby niece wailed piteously before their cries abruptly halted. It was then that Innes found her world spinning wildly and everything went dark.

She must have fainted for only a

short time because she came to her senses in time to hear the leader calling to his men. Dundallon was not to be put to the torch. The Queen ordered that the old tower-house and everything must be left as it was for the scavengers. The men were to be allowed their plunder and the scavengers would see to the rest.

Innes could hear their drunken cries as they shared out the wine and meat from the kitchens; she had already lost the contents of her own stomach and her gown was heavily soiled. In spite of the terrible nightmare and terror which had descended on her, she seemed to stand outside herself and forced herself to be calm and to remain perfectly still.

It seemed hours before the men were sated and they began to leave the great hall, singing and laughing drunkenly. The bodies of the people they had slain lay where they had fallen and for many minutes after they had gone, Innes continued to squat in her peephole, her legs refusing to move. The great hall was now dark with scarcely a candle left burning; and Innes wanted to scream and scream in sheer terror as she looked down on the vague outline of her once-beautiful sister-in-law. Archibald would be dead, too, and his children. He had helped to murder the King, and Queen Johanna had exacted a terrible punishment. Innes could hear, again, the red-faced man shouting out the tortures the Queen had caused to be inflicted on the culprits and that his own slaughter was quick and clean by comparison.

Clean! Innes shuddered and sickness overcame her again, then she crept out and went along to her own room, fearful of what she would find.

Janet Balfour lay on the floor, a trickle of blood soaking her skirts. Innes looked at her with horror but even as she looked, she could see the old woman stirring and she quickly knelt down beside her.

There was a pitcher of water on a table and Innes soaked a piece of linen and sponged the old woman's face. A moment later Janet began to thresh about, moaning faintly. Quickly Innes pulled at her skirts and examined the wound which had been intended as a fatal blow. It was only a flesh wound and Innes could see that Janet's voluminous skirts, and no doubt her age, had saved her. She bound up the wound, tearing off strips of clean linen from her shift which Janet had washed for her. The bleeding had stopped and as Innes again bathed her face, the old woman regained consciousness, only to screech loudly with terror.

'Hush your noise!' said Innes, sharply. 'At least you're alive, though I think we two must be the only ones left in the land of the living. They have put the household to the sword. They must have taken our guard by surprise . . . that would not be too difficult, since Archibald only left a few old men and boys to guard the castle.'

'Where is the master? And Lady Eleanor? What has happened to my lady?' Janet quavered.

'They are all dead,' Innes told her. 'They were put to the sword by a brute of a man whose thick fleshy face I shall never forget all the days of my life. I shall never forget him, or his men. Some day I shall avenge my brother's death, and my sister's and the children's.'

'The children!' moaned Janet. 'The bairns, too. But don't talk like that, Mistress Innes. There's been enough killing . . . I heard it all. I thought that surely you were dead, too. I remember it all now, and I thought my own end had come . . . '

Innes wiped her own face wearily. She allowed Janet to ramble on even as she pulled off her soiled clothing and began to dress in her warmest woollen skirts and thick cloak.

'Janet!' she said, urgently. 'Listen to me. We've got to get away from here. The scavengers are coming. Get yourself whatever clothing you need and we will leave Dundallon as soon as we can be on our way.'

'But where to, Mistress Innes?' Janet asked. 'I've never lived anywhere but Dundallon. My mother served Sir Archibald's grandfather till she was brought to bed.'

'Anywhere!' cried Innes, her nerves fraying, 'just be quiet and do as I say. We'll have to hide ourselves. We belong to Dundallon and if the Queen knew we were alive, we should soon be despatched. That soldier said she was mad with grief at the King's murder. We'll have to go where they won't find us. We'll go to your daughter's farm.'

'To Meg's! Oh no, Mistress Innes, that would surely not be right. Meg has only a poor farmstead and bairns to feed, and Thomas is a sour man.'

'She can hide us until we decide what to do,' said Innes, firmly. 'We can walk to Meg's'

'And let the soldiers put Meg and her bairns to the sword!' cried Janet, her eyes suddenly shrewd. 'No, Mistress Innes, we will not go to Meg's.'

'They will not think of looking for us there, I tell you,' said Innes, ruthlessly. 'We must go to Meg's.'

'No, Mistress Innes!'

'Very well. I shall snuff this candle and leave you to the scavengers who will be coming to bury the bodies. You can have them for company,' said Innes, cruelly. She was digging her nails into her palms to control herself and to give her courage to look upon the dead bodies in the great hall as something to be accepted without thinking too much about the people they had been when they were alive; all the people she had loved most in this world. Innes dared not think about them, or her brain would have turned.

'No, do not leave me with them.' Janet was crying. 'I canna look. I canna look on the dead or they'll haunt me all my days.'

'I'll haunt you all your days if you don't haste!' Innes muttered.

She had made a bundle of clothing and had thrown a warm cloak over her

18

shoulders and given her older one to Janet.

'Put that on. We'll take the candle and go to the kitchens to see if those beasts have left us any food.'

'I couldna eat!' Janet wailed.

'Meg cannot be expected to feed us. We will have to take food. And valuables. We will have to see if they have found Eleanor's hiding place for her best jewels, and we will bury the strongbox somewhere . . . in the woods, perhaps. I know where Archibald kept his merks for emergencies. We will take those, too. You carry this bundle and I will see to the rest. We've got to get away before the scavengers come, though maybe they will not be in any great hurry since they think we are all put to the sword. We will see if they have left a horse.'

'You are going mad, Mistress Innes . . . stealing my lady's jewels, and Sir Archibald's merks, and . . . food from the kitchen.'

'Should I leave it for the scavengers?'

asked Innes, harshly.

She had to cope with Janet's hysterics when they went down to the great hall and had to pick their way through the fallen victims and along the corridor to the kitchens. Innes made Janet stand outside in the cold night air, then she found food which had been overlooked by the men after they had shared out the wine. She also found Eleanor's strongbox and a purse of merks from a hidden hole near the fireplace in Archibald's room.

Out in the courtyard the air was clear and frosty and acted like a douche of cold water on Innes' face, though the queer unnatural silence which surrounded Dundallon was every bit as fearful as the cries of terror had been.

The moon had come up and the skies were clear of clouds so that an eerie blue light had been thrown over the old tower-house. Innes swallowed and chided Janet in order to still her own nerves.

'Pull your cloak tighter about you,'

she commanded. 'I shall see if those barbarians have left any of the horses. We cannot carry this food very far though I intend to hide our valuables until I can collect them in safety.'

'Suppose we . . . suppose they say we have stolen them,' mumbled Janet, whose greatest fear was that one day she would be accused of stealing. Hands had been cut off for less.

'You would be stealing from me, you fool!' said Innes, exasperated. 'With my brother and his family dead, I own Dundallon now.'

'Didna ye hear anything, Mistress? The Queen owns it now.'

'Stay there until I see if I can find a horse,' said Innes, anger beginning to boil in her. Why should the Queen own Dundallon? It was her — Innes' — home.

The stables were empty. There was a movement and a few sleepy squawks when Innes walked into the poultry house, though she drew back when she stumbled over the body of young Jamie

Cameron in the doorway. Here and there she could see dark shapes where men and boys had fallen, and her face felt clammy with sickness.

'Come on, nothing there,' she said to Janet. 'Thank God the drawbridge is down. We will make for the woods. then we will take the field paths to Meg's homestead. I will carry as much as I can.'

In the woods the darkness grew more intense, but Innes knew every blade of grass, every tree and shrub, and every stick and stone of the uneven ground. She knew she could not dig a hole to bury her valuables but she also knew exactly where to hide them; she leaned over the bank of a small stream, and put Eleanor's strong box, wrapped in one of her own well-darned shifts, into a recess just under the bank. The moon was throwing a ghostly blue light over the countryside and for a moment Innes wondered if she was being observed, but everything was still. She hesitated over the purse of merks, then decided to keep it.

'Come on,' she urged Janet. 'We'll keep close to the hedges in case the scavengers are mindful to come on the heels of the soldiers, though I doubt if they will travel until dawn. We must be under Meg's roof by then.'

The basket of food was heavy on her arm and when she carred it low, it knocked against her knees. Janet moaned beside her and Innes remembered that the old woman had been injured and was no doubt weak with pain and loss of blood. Suddenly her heart leapt as she heard a movement ahead of her, then the old donkey, Jinty, lumbered towards them.

'It's Jinty!' cried Innes. 'God be thanked. They have disdained old Jinty. Well, she's a mount fit for a princess tonight, Janet. Here, let me help you up.'

'Oh no, Mistress!' Janet quavered. 'I couldna ride while you walk.'

'You cannot walk,' said Innes in the same tone of voice. 'I will have no argument, old woman. I will help you on to Jinty and we will ride to Meg's in fine style. You can balance the basket and I'll carry our linen.'

As they put more and more distance between themselves and the horror they had left behind, Innes felt curiously light-headed. Almost she wanted to laugh and dance and sing, then sobs would rise up and choke her. Janet was almost in a fainting state, but Innes coaxed and cajoled the old woman, sometimes reminding her how lucky they were to have escaped, then making her stiffen up with fear that they were still in mortal danger.

It seemed like hours before the narrow path took a downward turn and again the moon came from behind the clouds to bathe the countryside in its strange blue light.

In a small valley they could see the outline of Meg Bell's farmstead which was little more than a hovel. The King had decreed that every farmer should dig a plot of land, seven feet long and six feet broad every working day if he were too poor to own an ox for ploughing; but Thomas Bell's plot often remained undug for many a day and Meg went in fear that he would be punished. He was a lazy man who had fathered four children, but could not even provide for a wife.

They would welcome the food, thought Janet, though Meg would not welcome Mistress Innes! And Janet did not trust Thomas. He would use the food and the coins and then what? Then he would not wish to feed two extra mouths!

'Not far now, Janet,' said Innes, trying to keep her voice cheerful though it was beginning to come out in a dragging croak. Her chest felt tight and her eyes stung and itched. She was tired and dirty, her gown bedraggled and her cloak covered with burrs.

'Try to hold on to the basket, Janet,' she urged.

But Janet had pulled up her donkey

and they were standing as still as a statue.

'Move, Janet! It is not far now!' cried Innes. 'What ails ye, woman?'

'Over there, Mistress Innes, over there!' Janet whispered.

Innes looked towards the hedgerows and suddenly the night, which had been as quiet as the grave, grew noisy with shrieks and howls.

'It's the beggars, Mistress,' sobbed Janet. 'We have fallen to the beggars.'

They were surrounded by a gang of ruffians, both men and women, whilst a hideous old man with white hair and a scrofulous face shouted instructions. They were surrounded by the gang, begging for alms. Innes quickly parted with her purse and her bundle of linen, whilst several of them begged for Janet's basket. Innes shrieked as she and Janet were separated and she could not see what was happening to the old woman.

'This one is a lady,' an old crone chuckled, gleefully. 'This one is worth a ransom.'

'We will take her with us, Hannah,' the whitehaired man commanded. 'Give her to Lizzie.'

Innes found her arm being taken in a vice-like grip by a girl only a few years older than herself, but she shuddered with revulsion at the sight of Lizzie. It was another nightmare into which she had fallen, but now shock and fatigue had dulled her senses, and she felt herself falling forward.

2

Innes did not know how long she had been unconscious but she woke to find the rhythmic movement of wheels beneath her and the cold night air with a sky full of stars above. A malodorous rug made of skins had been thrown over her, and the stench and rolling movement was enough to bring on an attack of nausea so that she retched over the side of the cart. Her stomach was empty, however, and a moment later a tall girl with long dark hair hanging about her shoulders came up to her. There had been a shawl round her head and now she pulled it close round her body.

'Ye can tak' a drink,' she conceded, handing Innes a flask. The girl drew back with distaste.

'I am well enough,' she muttered, though her mouth felt dry and swollen. 'Where am I?'

'Ye'll see soon enough,' the beggar girl said.

'Come away from there, Lizzie,' the old crone called. 'The maister will tell the lady if he wants her to be told anything.'

'I said nothing,' the girl replied, sulkily.

'Where is Janet Balfour?' Innes asked, weakly. 'Where is my . . . my companion?'

'I know naught,' the girl muttered.

Innes ran her hands over her body. Now that her bag of coins had gone, as had her change of clothing and the food, it was unlikely that the beggars would return her belongings so that her only possessions were the clothes she was wearing. She remembered that they were hoping to ransom her and smiled bitterly. Who would pay a ransom for her? There was no one in the world to whom she could turn.

Her heart quivered with fear when she thought that if she told the truth about herself, and informed the beggars that she belonged to Dundallon, they could perhaps collect even more money for handing a Frazer over to the Queen! She might be caught between Scylla and Charybdis!

They had turned in-country, well away from the sea. Innes lay and listened to the raucous talk of the beggars and could make little sense of it, though once or twice she imagined she could hear a well-modulated voice amongst them such as she might expect from a man of education.

She tried to twist round, but the band was straggled out and she could not see much beyond the plodding rump of the horse which pulled her cart. It appeared to be heaped with old clothes and food, and Innes remembered that no good housewife ever left her washing out to dry after dusk or it would be gone from sight by the time she remembered it.

Finally they were going down a narrow winding track between a belt of trees, and soon Innes could see the ruins of what must have been a castle as fine and well-appointed as Dundallon. Now it was a burned-out ruin, having no doubt been put to the torch.

The drawbridge was down and they all trundled over it, passing along the curtain wall and into the great hall, which was fairly weatherproof. It had been made into a communal enclosure for the beggars, and some had hung up skins and hides to give themselves privacy from a neighbour.

'The maister says we tak' her ben,' the old woman said. Innes' cart, which had been unhitched in the courtyard, was thrust into what remained of one of the curtain rooms, whilst she was hauled off with scant ceremony and made to walk along one of the corridors to a small apartment which had escaped most of the ravages of the rest of the castle. It contained little except a bed, a chair and one or two chests, and the bedding was similar to the rug which had covered her on the cart. Innes had expected to scratch herself free of vermin, but the rug, malodorous though it was, had been kept clear of the parasites. Now she was pushed on to the bed by the old woman, Hannah, where she cowered in fear. Was she to suffer the same fate as Eleanor, but this time at the hands of a scrofulous beggar? She could see the old woman grinning at her with only one or two teeth showing, and the girl, Lizzie, stared at her with bold curiosity.

'She is a lady,' the old woman grinned.

'Maybe,' Lizzie conceded, 'though her gowns are plain.'

'Warm wool. This cloak is fine. The maister was pleased with her purse. She will ransom.'

'I do not like ransom,' Lizzie muttered. 'They remember what they see.'

Innes was almost fainting again, this time through lack of food and water. She had thought that her stomach would revolt at the very thought of food after the horrors which had befallen her, but now she knew herself weak for food.

She tried to sit up but fell back on to the bed.

'What ails ye, Mistress?' the old woman asked.

'I . . . '

'She needs a bit of supper,' said a voice behind and the hideous leader of the beggars came in. 'See to it, Hannah, and you make up the fire, Lizzie Munro. We cannot have my hostage perishing before we can make use of her.'

'Aye, maister,' said Hannah whilst Lizzie gave the man a simpering smile. Innes was half fainting with revulsion as he came to look down on her.

'You look like a baby rabbit caught at the entrance to its burrow,' he said. 'You could stand looking at it all day long and it would give you stare for stare, absolutely petrified. Did you know that, Mistress? Or is it My Lady?'

'Where is Janet Balfour, you horrible smelly old man?' she demanded.

She had been through so much that was fearful that she hardly cared any more.

'Ah . . . not quite the rabbit,' he amended. 'The old woman? Is she your serving woman . . . your maidservant?'

'She could be my mother.'

'You must not try to tell me lies, or think to throw me off the scent. I know I have a young lady as my guest and that your old woman has been a servant all her life. She is safe enough.'

'Ask her about me then.'

'She is a stubborn woman but I might learn from her if . . . if I tortured her just a wee bit . . . '

She thought there was a gleam in his eyes.

'No!' she cried. 'Don't you dare lay a finger on her. I'll see you hang . . . '

She broke off. She was in no position to see anyone hang.

'Then who are you?' he asked, silkily.

'I am fainting with hunger, sir,' she said, changing her tack. 'I was going to stay with Janet's daughter. My . . . my parents have died.'

'And your relatives?'

'I have none.'

'Your name?'

'Innes . . . ' she began, ' . . . Jane Innes.'

'Jane Innes,' he repeated, frowning. There was no family by that name near Dundallon, but he appeared to believe her. No doubt Janet had raved about 'Mistress Innes.'

'My brother and sister-in-law have died and I was left with a . . . ' she was about to say a small amount of money but decided to amend this, ' . . . left with a fortune, sir. It was all in my purse which you have taken from me. It was a great deal of money, sir, and all I had in the world.'

He made no reply.

'And you lived . . . where?'

'Near Dundallon, on the coast. My brother caught fish and sold the catch. Janet Balfour helped to nurse my sister-in-law, and was going home now that my family are all dead. I cannot pay her because I need to find a husband with a fortune. It is all I have.'

The piercing eyes stared at her from the horribly-marked face.

'Hm. I do not believe you,' he said at length. 'You are lying. But I will find out the truth sooner or later. Ah, here is some broth for you. Eat it up and it will bring back your strength.'

The soup was as rough as the beggars themselves, and Innes wanted to make a face of distaste, but she did not dare. He was watching her closely, so she smiled and nodded.

'Good soup.'

She drank a little more.

'You are lying to me,' he repeated, very softly, 'and I shall have the truth of it, never fear.'

As he went out Innes reflected on the last sentence or two. At first the beggar lord had spoken in a gruff, raucous voice like the other beggars, but it had gradually changed to the well-modulated voice she had heard before. He was master of the beggars, but he was also a fraud, being no more beggar than she was the sister of a fisherman. At some time in his life he had been a gentleman, though it was not difficult to see why he had chosen to live, now, in this twilight world. He was surely the most hideous man she had ever seen.

*   *   *

For a few days Innes was kept away from the band of beggars, though she could hear the noisy laughter of the men and shrill voices of the women as they shouted at their fractious children. They appeared to be rebuilding part of the ruined castle because Innes could hear, faintly, the sounds of stone masons at work. Perhaps their plunder was being spent on restoring this castle for them to inhabit, thought Innes, and she wondered if her purse of merks would add to their industry.

Smaller bands of beggars left each evening at twilight to return, sometimes before midnight, and sometimes not until dawn. They brought game a-plenty and

Innes was served often with a pot stew which was nourishing if rough fare. Her body began to gather strength, though, as her senses grew less numb, so did her fear grow greater. What would they do with her when they found out who she was? They had horses and wagons and their leader, or 'the maister' as they referred to him, had ridden away shortly after Innes was captured and had not yet returned. She had no doubt at all that he was making enquiries about her.

The weather remained cold and frosty, and, one morning, Hannah Munro and Lizzie came to find Innes and to throw a dirty, bedraggled gown on to the bed and an ancient shawl to cover her head.

'She will have to dirty up her white face and hands,' said Hannah, leering into Innes' face.

'What for?' the girl asked, fearfully. 'What are you going to do with me?'

'Put ye tae work, of course,' said Lizzie. 'You don't think you can lie here being fed like a turkey cock and not earn your meat. You'll beg like the rest o' us.'

'Beg! But . . . but I cannot beg!' cried Innes, horrified.

'Why not?'

'I . . . I have no licence. It is the law. One must have a licence to beg.'

'And how many of us stick to the law?' asked Lizzie.

'But . . . but you must stick to the law,' said Innes, 'else you will have your cheek branded.'

She put a hand up to her own soft cheek as though she were already feeling the heat from a branding-iron.

'Who is going to arrest us?' asked Lizzie, scornfully. 'We are a band, are we not? We are not some old beggar working on his own. So get up and put these on, Mistress, then I'll dae ye up so that your own mother would not know ye. We cannot go showing your soft pale face to the nobles or they would have neither fear nor respect for you. No one denies Ma here, when the mood is on her.'

Hannah cackled with pride. 'Nor you, Lizzie, nor you! The men are looking twice at you.'

Lizzie's face darkened. 'They know not to lay a finger on me. I am not their property.'

'Na, but ye tak' their property,' screeched Hannah, delighted with her own joke.

'We are wasting time,' said Lizzie, impatiently. 'Help me to tie this round the ransom maid.'

She put the voluminous dress on to Innes, then tied it at the waist with a piece of rope. With the shawl it all smelled abominably and Innes felt her stomach growing queasy again. It brought back renewed memories of Eleanor and the terrible night which sometimes seemed years away.

Innes felt a great surge of grief in her heart, but she had to force it down again. She dared not think about her family.

'I hold the rope,' said Lizzie, grimly. 'It will keep our own men from fondling you and you will not want to run away, will you? Whatever you were, you are a beggar maid now.'

Innes shuddered as she was pushed amongst a band of other women whose dirty appearance and unkempt hair seemed to have been made filthier with wood ash and herbal juices, some of which were now rubbed into Innes' face and smeared on to her hands and arms. Then, almost fainting again with fear and revulsion, she was forced to run with the beggars, waylaying travellers, who quickly parted with some of their belongings. The band had been warned that they must not rob, only beg.

Innes noticed that the mulcted ones did not lose all they possessed and wondered if this was a ploy to avoid capture. The victims were consoled a little by being allowed to keep some of their treasures and appeared to consider that, instead of being robbed, they had given alms to the poor.

'Bless you, sir, bless you, mistress,' the beggars would whine. 'Alms for the poor. Feed the starving . . . ye will not be wanting this poor bit o' siller. A fine burgess like yersel will have plenty more at home.'

Innes was given a great poke in the ribs and told to whine with the women. She did so, almost automatically, being in a fair mood to whine for a short while, and finding the keening strangely hypnotic. Then the anger and rebellion in her nature came to the fore and when Lizzie would have thrust her forward again, Innes turned on her almost savagely so that the beggar girl drew back, and one or two others showed respect.

'I will not!' she hissed, 'and you cannot force me. I will talk to your leader when he returns, but I will beg no more for you.'

'You have already begged for us,' Lizzie said, a gleam of malice in her eyes. 'You are no better than the rest of us. You are a beggar maid.'

Innes did not reply. Already the party was returning to the old ruin with their spoils thrown into the cart; but she was given a fine silk shawl to carry and told to keep it clean. It still seemed to be warm and faintly perfumed from the body of the lady who had handed it over. Innes and she had stared at one another for a long moment and Innes could see contempt in the other's eyes. So might she have treated the beggars at one time, and now she was one of them.

Hot tears mingled with the sticky herbal juices and wood ash which had been rubbed into her face, so that she knew she must look as ill-kempt and hideous as the rest of the women. Then again anger bit into her.

'I will not go snivelling,' she told herself. 'I will not! They can't make me, not those beasts of soldiers, not these horrible beggars, not even the Queen. No one is going to make me weep with weakness or grovel for mercy. I am Mistress Innes Frazer. I shall tell their leader my true name, and he can do what he will.'

She muttered the words under her breath and glanced at Lizzie, who glared back.

There was a trough of water in the courtyard and Innes ran forward and splashed the water on to her face and hands, rubbing them vigorously even though the chill of the water struck ice into her heart. Old Hannah had grabbed the silk shawl with loud cries of protest, and Lizzie rushed over to order Innes back to her room.

'I will go when I am clean,' she said, calmly, 'and not one minute before.'

'You will go when I tell you,' Lizzie panted.

'I refuse to do anything you tell me.'

'Lizzie's bony fist smashed into her ear so that Innes reeled with pain. Quickly she rallied and before she could think better of it, she had pushed Lizzie into the trough of water.

There was a queer silence amongst the beggars, then they began to gather as Lizzie heaved herself out of the water, coughing and spluttering.

'A good bath will not come amiss,' Innes taunted though her knees were shaking with fright. It was dark but the beggars had brought torches so that the courtyard was lit up. Would she have to kick and claw, push and bite at Lizzie just to prove that she was not a weakling and desired to be left alone? She would, indeed, be reduced to the level of beggar maid if she had to fight like a cat for her independence.

Then suddenly a tall figure, surrounded by a band of ruffians, hove into sight; and although he was a mere shadow in the darkness, Innes soon recognised the 'maister's' voice.

'What is the meaning of this?' he bellowed. 'Do I have to beat you women in order to discipline you? God's truth, is it the captive? What is she doing out of her apartment?'

'Lizzie made her beg, maister,' said old Hannah, not averse to 'clyping', even against her own daughter.

'I gave orders that she was to be kept to her room,' the leader said, furiously, his eye, hideously puckered, running over the two girls. Water dribbled from Lizzie's skirts and Innes was shaking the wood ash from her hair. 'Get inside, Mistress. You will remain in your room until I have time to talk to you. And you, Lizzie Munro, I will see you after sunrise.'

'Yes, Maister,' said Lizzie, through chattering teeth.

She glanced at Innes, then clattered along the stone corridor towards the great hall.

'See the captive to her room,' the leader commanded, turning to Hannah.

'Aye, Maister,' she acknowledged. 'Come along wi' me, Mistress. Ye canna leave your room now that the maister is back.'

* * *

Innes had expected an early visit the following morning but only Hannah came to attend to her and to bring her a hot drink made out of warmed wine, sweetened with honey.

'It will tak' the chill from yer bones,' the old woman said, 'and ye should eat yer oatmeal. Ye canna get ill or the ransom will be smaller, and the maister will not want a sickly woman on his hands.'

In fact, Innes felt much fresher for the night out in the fresh air, hideous though it was. She would think of it as a Hallows Eve ploy or a romp after a wolf hunt. She would not believe that it had all been real and earnest.

Lizzie did not come near her, and once she thought she could hear a woman crying angry tears. Innes' heart softened. Lizzie was probably living the only kind of life she knew.

It was late afternoon when the master finally arrived and ordered Hannah from the room with admonitions that, if she were found trying to listen at the door, she would be soundly beaten.

'I won't listen, Maister,' she promised. 'I will go and seek poor Lizzie.'

'She disobeyed me,' the master said,

grimly. 'I will not have disobedience from a single one of you. Understand?'

'Yes, Maister,' Hannah whispered, and scuttled from the room.

After Hannah had gone, the beggar lord stood in front of Innes, who had scrambled up to a sitting position on the side of the bed. She was almost fainting again with revulsion. Surely the moment had come when she would be helpless against this horrible old man, with nowhere to run and no one to protect her. Almost she wished she had shared the same fate as Eleanor.

'Well, Mistress Frazer, so you have been lying to me,' he said at length and her face paled when she realised that he had learned her identity.

'If you know so much, you will also know that I have no one to pay ransom for me,' she said, defiantly.

'The Queen might like to know that you are still in the land of the living,' he said, softly, sitting down on a large chest which had been shoved against a wall.

She pushed her hair out of her eyes tiredly.

'Why do you not proceed with what you have to do?' she asked, with dignity. 'My brother helped to murder the King and we deserve punishment.'

'Except that your brother took against King James because the King punished his mother's kith and kin for supporting the Duke of Albany, the King's uncle and Regent of Scotland, while James was imprisoned in England. James never forgave his uncle for not paying a ransom to get him home; and, when he was allowed to come home and to claim his crown, his first task was to execute his cousin, Duke Murdoch, and his family, and punish those who had sided with him. Sir Archibald Frazer's mother was a Cunningham and the Cunninghams were all punished, which made Sir Archibald the King's enemy. Your mother was Mistress Jane Innes, who had no quarrel with the King, yet you are now a marked woman for what your brother did. Life is very unfair, is it not, Mistress Frazer?'

Innes swallowed. 'How . . . how did you learn all this?' she asked, curious in spite of herself. She found that she could listen with ease to the beggar lord's voice if she did not have to look at his face.

'My father was Master Robert Stewart, kinsman to King James and he, too, was Albany's man. You are now at Invernairn, my father's property which was destroyed by the King, and my father lost his head. I was his heir . . . heir to this . . . '

He threw out a gloved hand and waved it around contemptuously.

'Then . . . then you are . . . '

'Ruari Stewart, at your service, Mistress,' he said, making her a slight bow. 'My cousin is head of our family, Sir Alexander Stewart of Glenallyn, one-time friend to your brother until he learned what he was up to. Alexander is not a fool. He declared himself a King's man as soon as James showed himself to be a fine strong King and well able to punish anyone who disagreed with him. My cousin knows when to be . . . ah . . . circumspect. He remembered your family and has met your father and mother, your brother and sister-in-law, and he remembered that there was a stepchild somewhere . . . yourself, Mistress Innes Frazer.'

'I do not remember him,' said Innes, coldly. How could she tell whether this beggar lord was speaking the truth or not? He might have obtained his information from the soldiers.

'He is a tall dark man with very black hair, much like myself,' Ruari Stewart said, casually lifting off the evil-looking wig which adorned his head and pulling at the horrible disguise which hid his face. He stood up and shed the repulsive garments which had turned him into a beggar lord, and smoothed down the garnet-coloured velvet waistcoat and fine wool shirt which he wore underneath.

Innes could not restrain a gasp of

sheer incredulity as she stared at him. Never before had she seen a more handsome man. He was peeling off the gloves which covered his white slender hands, after which he smiled at her, his black eyes bright and merry as a cricket.

'If I must be a beggar, I must look the part,' he remarked.

'But . . . but I don't understand . . . '

'Don't you?' There was a touch of merriment in his eyes as he gazed at her. 'Invernairn is mine! The King turned it into a ruin and his good subjects allowed it to happen, so now they are going to put it all back for me.'

'But . . . but that can't be right,' she protested. 'You cannot rob people just to build up your property again.'

'Who says that I rob? I *beg*, Mistress Innes,' he insisted. 'How are we to live . . . the servants and I? They were lucky to escape with their lives. My father did not play a big part against the King, so James was lenient with him and I escaped with my life, as did my servants. Only Invernairn suffered. But the Queen was not so lenient with Dundallon, was she?'

Innes' eyes darkened with pain as she shook her head.

'My servants are still alive, and must be fed so that they can build themselves a home again. They will till the soil once more when Invernairn is back on its feet.'

'They will not!' she cried, her eyes flashing. 'Don't you see that they are turning themselves into real beggars? You have taught them to beg, and how to waylay travellers and coax and whine, but you will never turn them away from it. When a man turns beggar, he will not go back to hard toil again.'

'That is enough!' he said, and this time there was a flush on his cheeks. 'What do you know about it? You are a mere child . . . a young maid. You will have learned nothing about life, until now. But now you are going to learn a great deal.'

She shrank from him, even though

his looks were now enough to turn the head of any woman. Innes had stared at him with fascination, but she was still repelled by his nature. He was still a beggar.

'What are you going to do with me?' she whispered.

'Declare that you belong to me,' he said, his eyes gleaming a little. 'There are men out there who would enjoy a captive maid if she had nothing to offer but herself.'

'I had my purse,' she cried. 'You stole it.'

'Begged it. Not a very big purse,' he said. 'It's in safe keeping.' He shook his head, his eyes dancing again. 'Even though you tried to tell me that it was your fortune from your poor fisherman brother, or some such relative. Oh, dear Mistress Innes, you are not above spinning a few tales yourself.'

She made no reply and he stared at her for a long moment. 'Have you no relatives, no kith or kin? Why were you going to that farmstead hovel when we found you?'

'Where is Janet?' she asked.

'She is safe.'

'Thank God for that. It . . . it was the only place I could think of. Dundallon was . . . '

'I have seen Dundallon,' he nodded, his voice suddenly gentle.

'There was only Meg Bell and Leyburn.'

He got up to saunter round the room.

'You cannot stay here,' he said at length. 'I will have to make other arrangements for you. Meanwhile . . . meanwhile they will all have to know you are my woman . . . '

He threw open the door and dragged her up, putting his arm round her tightly and leading her along the corridor towards the great hall, where he stopped and pulled her into his arms, kissing her fiercely.

Innes struggled. She had never been kissed by a man before, but for a brief peck on the cheek from Archibald, and now her body seemed to turn to water so that she stopped struggling. Her heart was pounding madly and she could feel the power and strength of Ruari Stewart as he held her against him.

Suddenly he looked round, seeing that several of the beggars were eyeing them with interest.

'She is my woman, you understand?' he cried. 'No one touches her but me. D'ye hear?'

'Aye, Maister,' they mumbled and he roared the question again so that they all answered loudly and clearly.

Ruari grabbed Innes and pulled her round once more to return her to her room but she caught sight of Lizzie's face and it was black with hatred.

'You will stay here until I know what to do with you,' he commanded. 'Hannah Munro and Lizzie will attend you.'

'Do they know who I am?' she whispered. She did not trust Lizzie who might easily find the soldiers for her.

'They do not. They are only told

what is good for them to hear. They are servants of Invernairn ... most of them,' he added, carelessly. 'They will expect me to sleep with you.'

She shrank at the bald statement and he gave her a smile of devilment.

'Do not fret, Mistress Innes, I have to do a great deal of beggaring at nights.'

3

The next week or two seemed like a long waiting period in Innes' life. She learned from Hannah that Janet Balfour had been escorted to her daughter's home at Leyburn along with most of the food they had brought out of Dundallon.

'Surely she will be anxious for me,' said Innes, fretfully.

'Not Mistress Balfour!' grinned Hannah. 'She thinks you have been sent to live with noble friends and who is more noble than the maister?'

Lizzie glared at her mother and darted a venomous glance at Innes. Surely the girl could not be jealous of her! When she combed her hair and put on a clean gown, well above her station, she was a comely woman who had no doubt warmed her lord's bed. She took no heed of breaking the law, which not only decreed that a beggar should be licensed but also that no one except a lord or a knight could wear silks or furs. Even the farmer had to wear plain homespun, yet Lizzie enjoyed decking herself in the rich gowns which had been plundered, or coaxed as Innes remembered, from luckless travellers.

Innes was sharply aware of the state of her own clothing. They had been soiled and muddied and she would have given much for Janet to be nearby, bathing her in warm scented water and holding out a pretty gown for her to wear. Friends calling on Eleanor had said that the Queen and her ladies wore finely-woven silks, with pretty head-dresses, but then, the Queen was English and had learned her manners at the English court.

Thinking about the Queen, Innes' mouth went dry and she turned over in her mind the snippets of news which Ruari Stewart had given her. The lady was demented with rage and grief, he said. The King had gone to Blackfriars monastery at Perth, with a number of courtiers, in order to have a rest from his responsibilities and to play some of the outdoor games which he loved.

In particular, he had enjoyed several games of tennis, but had caused a hole to be blocked up to prevent his tennis balls from being lost. Later he had great cause to regret this small, seemingly trifling incident; when, one evening as he relaxed with the Queen and her ladies, playing the lute and reciting poems which he had written himself, Sir Robert Graham and a party of men had broken into the chamber.

'Lady Catherine Douglas was very brave, as I understand it,' Ruari Stewart told her. 'Sir Robert Stewart, the King's chamberlain and one of my own kinsmen, had destroyed all the locks . . . there's treachery for you, if you like . . . and Lady Catherine rushed to put her arm through the lock while the King was lowered into an underground passage. Had he not blocked up that hole, he would have got away.'

'And Lady . . . Lady Catherine . . . '

'Her arm was broken,' said Ruari, almost carelessly, though she could see the firming of his mouth. He had not liked the King's murder any more than she did herself. It was a cowardly murder and she was ashamed that Archibald had played a part in it. She suspected that Ruari Stewart was also ashamed that he, too, had a kinsman who was involved. Yet why should she attribute any finer feelings to him when he lived this careless life, begging from decent citizens? Why should she give him any respect, or sit listening to his every word? Yet she often longed for his return and to hear whatever news he could bring.

'The Queen has gone to Edinburgh,' he told her one evening, 'and the new King, James II, is to be crowned at the Chapel of Holyrood instead of Scone. He is only six years old, so we are in for a restless time until he grows up and proves himself as big a man as his father. God knows I had no call to love the man, but I could not but respect him. He was the King and he ruled like a King, and woe betide anyone who crossed him. 'A rotten apple ruins the barrel', he used to say and he would chop out the rotten apple. Yet the poor people could always petition him for their rights. It is ironical — is it not? — that he would have listened to Ruari Stewart, beggar, before he would listen to the petition of Master Ruari Stewart of Invernairn.'

'I cannot believe that he is dead,' said Innes, 'and that my brother was concerned in it.'

'If he had not been concerned in it, you would be asleep in your little cot now instead of dropping into the clutches of the Invernairn beggars, and one in particular.'

His eyes gleamed into hers so that her heart began to race again. This spell of being left to her own devices would not last for ever, then what would happen? Would ... would Master Stewart try to force her? She thought she could see amusement in the look he cast at her, though she was too apprehensive to care.

'Who will rule the country?' she asked, hurriedly, hoping to divert him. 'Surely the Queen will not be Regent?'

'The Queen!' cried Ruari, diverted instantly. 'A demented woman! No, the Queen is certainly not fit to run the country. It takes a man, and a strong man, to do that. Earl Douglas has the authority at the moment, but I do not like the way that Chrichton and Livingstone keep snarling at one another like a couple of dogs over a bone. Sir William Chrichton is the Governor of Edinburgh Castle and openly declared himself for the Queen since he was a great friend to King James, but Livingstone will not let things rest there.'

'Why?' asked Innes. 'What could he do?'

'Get hold of the boy King's person, by fair means or foul,' said Ruari. 'The one who holds the King's person wields the most power.'

'You mean kidnap the King?' asked Innes, her eyes wide.

'I do not know what I mean,' said Ruari, 'and you ask too many questions for a young maid. We could entertain one another in a better way than discussing the state of our poor country. I found your lips sweet and fresh when I showed my band of beggars that I laid claim to you, Mistress Innes. I would fain return for another taste of the honey.'

He stood up and came over to stand beside her, then his nose wrinkled.

'Lord'a'mercy, but your garments are not as sweet as your face,' he said. 'What ails ye that ye have not changed out of your soiled linen?'

'Only that I have no other to wear, sir,' she said, the colour burning bright in her face and anger sparking from her eyes. 'If you do not remember, I will refresh your memory. My nurse and I were set upon by a band of robbers and I have lost all my garments but what I stand up in.'

Master Stewart drew himself up very tall and his face grew dark as thunder.

'Hannah Munro!' he called, 'and you . . . Lizzie Munro! Come here at once.'

The old woman hurried in so quickly that Innes suspected her ear had been close to the door again. Lizzie sauntered in at a more leisurely pace. She had washed and combed her hair so that Innes could see that it shone with dark blue lights. She had draped the soft shawl Innes had carried home over her shoulders and smiled invitingly at the master.

Innes felt sure that they were lovers, and a queer feeling lay in her heart like a sickness, almost as though she were disappointed, or even jealous. But that could not be true, she thought. How could she be jealous of a beggar? Because whatever Ruari Stewart had been, he was now a beggar.

'I gave you orders to return the clothing to Mistress . . . Mistress Innes,' he said.

Innes moved restlessly, but she was

relieved that he had made no mention of the name 'Frazer'.

'It got mixed up with other garments,' said Lizzie, shrugging.

Master Stewart caught her arm in a vicelike grip, his eyes snapping with anger.

'I will not listen to lies,' he hissed. 'Go and bring that clothing, and give it to this lady. You, Hannah, go and warm up water so that she may bathe. She is dirty.'

'Enough water to bath her, Maister, like . . . like you have yourself?'

'Exactly like I have myself.'

'It's a lot o' water from the well, Maister.'

'Then the quicker you get started, the better. Get another woman to help you. I will not have my . . . my woman in a dirty state.'

Innes' cheeks were like twin fires. Not only had she the indignity of being considered dirty, but Master Stewart kept referring to her as his 'woman'.

She was not his woman! she thought

rebelliously, and he would not take her, even if he almost killed her in the attempt.

'Wash the ashes out of your hair,' he said as he left the room. 'You look like a beggar maid!'

★ ★ ★

Unwilling though she was to attend to Innes, Lizzie nevertheless obeyed the master and helped her mother to prepare a bath for Innes, and to return her bundle of clothing. From the selection of garments which she had packed, Innes chose clean linen and a fur-trimmed gown embroidered with pearls. Her hair was carefully washed and dried so that it fell in rich dark red curls about her shoulders. She had brought no ornament to wear, but she felt clean and neat once more.

Lizzie's lip curled a little as she looked at her.

'You're a poor bit thing,' she commented, 'no decent flesh on ye at all. I tell ye, it takes more than a milksop to satisfy the maister.'

'Haud yer wheesht!' Hannah cautioned. 'Yer tongue will be the death of ye yet, our Lizzie.'

'And you are too humble, old woman,' cried Lizzie. 'My father was a decent farmer who lost his land when Invernairn was taken by the Crown. He was killed in the fighting. But you . . . you forget you were a farmer's wife, and a free woman. You've become a real beggar.'

'What else are you, Lizzie Munro?'

'A lot else. I pull my weight with the best of them and I can be a beggar on top. But underneath . . . inside . . . I am as good as any hereabouts.'

She stared at Innes as though daring her to deny it. But Innes could only think about her own fate. What was to become of her now that Archibald had smirched their name? She smoothed down the gown and picked up a soft cream shawl. It seemed ridiculous to dress up in finery in such a place as this ruin which had been Invernairn, but just for once she would obey the master's wishes.

Hannah and Lizzie had barely cleared away the bath water and discarded garments when Ruari Stewart's firm tread resounded along the corridor. Innes recoiled though she found her heart beating with excitement. What would Ruari think of her now? It would be the first time he had ever seen her out of her rags; and, if Innes had been honest with herself, she would have had to admit that she chose her fine clothes with a view to impressing the master as to her looks and bearing. She had grown taller than average and her dark red hair and amber eyes had been a legacy from the Frazers, though her features and figure had been inherited from her mother. She had often heard it said that her mother was very beautiful, and Eleanor had remarked on Innes' looks after she had turned sixteen.

Now she rose to her feet and turned

to face Master Stewart as he strode into the room, and for a long moment they regarded one another. Ruari's eyes swept over her slowly and deliberately, and now and again he nodded.

'Not bad,' he conceded. 'Not bad at all.'

She went scarlet with anger, and her amber eyes sparked with green lights.

'You look at me as though I . . . I were horseflesh you wished to sell, Master Stewart.'

Again the gleam of amusement and perhaps a little more was back in his eyes.

'Have patience, Mistress,' he said, soothingly. 'I declare you are a mettlesome lady. Now I will be away for a few days and you are free to wander around Invernairn or what is left of it, so long as you do not attempt to leave. I will not have you wandering about on your own or you might meet with a worse fate than the one I hope to arrange for you. Have I your promise that you will not run away, or be a nuisance to my servants when I have gone? Every one of them has his, or her, work to do at Invernairn. They do not spend all their time on the road.'

'I am glad to hear it,' she said, disdainfully, so that he took a step towards her, his young face suddenly harsh with anger.

'Do not try me, Mistress, or I might discard the plans I am trying to make for your welfare, and adopt another which takes care of my own,' he said, warningly, 'and it would be less to the liking of a lady, I assure you.'

She drew back at the anger in his voice.

'Your word, as a lady, to me,' he insisted.

'My word, Master Stewart.'

He nodded, then quickly left the chamber, his feet resounding in the corridor. Illogically she felt almost sick with disappointment and wanted to rip the pretty gown from her back and stamp it under her feet. Then her cheeks burned when she thought about the times she had behaved in just such a fashion, giving work and troubles to old Janet. Innes could feel the tears of shame and mortification stinging her eyelids.

Slowly she walked over to where her clothing had been laid out on another chest. Selecting a warm woollen gown of a rustic shade which she had often worn at Dundallon, she began to unhook the heavy silk, struggling to reach the back hooks without calling for Hannah or Lizzie Munro. She wanted no service from them. She had been perfectly correct in what she told Ruari Stewart that beggaring would turn his servants into true beggars, and that included himself! He had no notion how to comport himself like a gentleman.

She struggled into the older gown and laid the fur-trimmed one away. When would she wear it again, if ever? She had given her word that she would not run away, the word of a lady to a gentleman. Yet . . . he was not a gentleman, she thought angrily . . . so her word was not binding. She might seize her chance and leave . . .

But where could she go? Who would give her shelter? And suppose she fell in with a band of true beggars who had no need of disguise to give them evil looks. She might not fare so well amongst them! Ruari was quite right when he pointed this out to her.

Innes kicked and scuffed with her feet, greatly at odds with herself; and when she dared search in her heart for a reason, she could not but see that she was ill pleased because Ruari Stewart had not admired her more. Her cheeks burned at the thought! No wonder Eleanor had been remarking quite often to Archibald that he should find a husband for his sister and that she was 'ripe for it'.

At least she had given no hint of her feelings to him, thought Innes, taking herself firmly in hand. She was indeed lost if all she wanted in life was to seek the favours of a beggar lord! And one who took such as Lizzie to bed!

She could hear the noise of the beggars from the great hall and the smell of cooking venison stew. Sometimes she longed for dainties such as honey cakes or the delicately spiced foods that Eleanor had taught the cooks to provide at Dundallon, and she would have given much for a small slice of bread with her meat, but this was a delicacy which was not shared with the common people. They ate their meat without such niceties.

Hannah shuffled along the corridor with a platter of stew, and Innes felt like rejecting it haughtily, then changed her mind. Her appetite had grown healthy again even though sometimes it lay sour on her stomach when thoughts of Dundallon crowded into her mind. But she was becoming adept at pushing such thoughts well below the surface. She could only tolerate being alive if she tried not to remember an existence previous to the one she was living with Ruari Stewart's beggars.

'So your finery did not last long,'

Hannah cackled. 'The winds blaw snell from the east, Mistress, and ye will not be dancing at the ball.'

She shouted with laughter at her own drollery, so that Innes longed to box her ears as she would have done Janet's.

'Hold your tongue, old woman,' she said, crossly. 'You cackle like a laying hen.'

'Mind yersel' wi' Lizzie,' the old woman said, in a loud whisper. 'She's like her faither. She'll clype on ye, Mistress, if she's a mind.'

'Who to? About what?' asked Innes, half fearfully, but the old woman would not be drawn.

'I've brought you some warm ale,' she said, ingratiatingly. 'Remember that auld Hannah helped ye.'

She leered and Innes hardly knew which was most distasteful — Lizzie's jealous hatred or the old woman's sickly fawning.

★   ★   ★

The beggars eyed Innes warily when she walked out amongst them, feeling that the small chamber was like a prison; since she had no reason to fear the beggar gang, she might find interest in studying the kind of lives they lived. For once Lizzie forgot her jealousy and talked with her, and it was from Lizzie that she learned that Ruari had sworn an oath of fealty to the new King James II; and had been granted his lands back again, even though he would have to restore Invernairn himself.

Work was now going ahead openly, and the beggars were more like servants as they cleaned the walls and spread rushes on the floors of some of the apartments which had already been made water-tight.

The roof was being replaced, and already some of the labourers' dwellings were being rebuilt with turf. Ox-hides would serve for doors until the houses could be improved.

'Some day the labourers' cottages will be built of stone, like town houses today,' said Innes, thinking that she would have little stomach for a turf house with an ox-hide for a door.

Lizzie shrugged. 'They are well enough. What labourer has time to sit inside his hovel and enjoy its finery?' she asked, contemptuously.

'Life is so unfair,' said Innes, 'when some people are so poor while others ... ' She hesitated, remembering that she was now as poor as anyone.

'The Maister will soon build up Invernairn again,' said Lizzie. 'The farmers will dig their plots and kill the crows, and shoot their arrows every holiday at the target near the church door, but some of them are now too fond of begging, and they will keep to the band.'

'Begging is illegal for people between the ages of fourteen and seventy,' said Innes. 'I remember my ... I remember learning about that law,' she amended having almost told Lizzie about Archibald! She would have to guard her tongue. Lizzie, showing a friendly spirit, was even more dangerous than when her eyes spat hatred.

'Where did ye learn it?' Lizzie was asking, casually.

'From my father,' said Innes, after a pause.

'Where is he? Is he exiled?'

'No, he's dead . . . and my mother. I have no one. I was on my way to an old farmstead to stay with a . . . a friend when you captured me.'

'Is the friend a nobleman?'

'No, she is the wife of a farmer . . . a free man.'

'Then you are no better than I am,' cried Lizzie in triumph.

'No better at all,' Innes agreed pleasantly.

'Then keep away from the maister wi' yer fancy ways,' said Lizzie. 'Ye had best be back in your apartment. Not that I want ye here, but the maister might turn against me if ye are not here when he returns.'

Innes turned about feeling that the

mood had altered between them. Lizzie was torn between pleasure that she was a mere nobody and contempt that she was being asked to look after that same nobody.

Innes returned to her room and thought a little more about Ruari Stewart. There was no longer any need for him to be in hiding. If what Lizzie said was true, he was a free man and sworn to the new King.

'Master Ruari Stewart of Invernairn,' she whispered to herself.

It had a fine ring to it.

4

Ruari Stewart rode back to Invernairn a sennight later and Innes' heart leapt when she heard the sounds of the horsemen riding in.

There was little of the beggar now in his wearing apparel and that of his henchmen, and it was apparent that he had been out on more lawful business.

Innes kept to her chamber, determined that she would not run out and show her pleasure in the master's return. She would not rival Lizzie for his favours! She listened to the sounds of revelry and knew that food and drink was being served to the men and the minutes seemed to drag past. Finally, she was forced to go to bed knowing that the master had no intention of calling in to talk to her that evening. She should be glad, she assured herself, that she did not have to talk to her captor or be troubled by him; but, instead, she could have wept with frustration and anger that he could choose to ignore her like this. Was she such a nonentity that she could be thrust to the back of his mind? Was food and drink so much more important to him than her welfare? Perhaps he might even have to be reminded that he held her imprisoned in Invernairn.

As she lay on her bed she was sure that she heard shrill laughter and she clenched her fists, wondering if Lizzie's comforts had been sought by the master. In spite of his new finery, he was just a beggar at heart, she thought, as was Lizzie. They were not worthy of her musings.

★ ★ ★

It was two days before Ruari came to see her, bearing with him her purse of merks which he placed beside her where she sat by a small window and mended a petticoat she had torn whilst walking amongst the briars.

'Hannah will pack your belongings, Mistress Innes,' he said without preliminary. 'We will leave at an early hour in the morning.'

'Where do we go, sir?' she asked with alarm.

'Rest content,' he told her, impatiently. 'I have not betrayed you to the enemies of your brother. I do not consider that they are your enemies.'

'Then what will you do with me?'

'As much as I would do for my own sister, or for any young woman,' he told her. 'I have found you a home, second to none, and I have done all that your brother would have done for you.'

Innes stared at him.

'I still do not understand.'

'He would have arranged a match for you,' said Ruari Stewart, 'would he not? You are old enough and ready for marriage, I am quite sure.'

She grew scarlet at his tone. It seemed to put her in the same category as a fine ripe plum from the orchard.

'Sir, my brother had not time to arrange a match for me,' she said, with dignity. 'It was never discussed.'

'No, he had his own affairs to settle first of all,' said Ruari, grimly. 'Well, what else can I do with a lady of your standing? Have you hired out as a servant? Join the band who wish to continue as beggars? . . . Oh yes, you were right up to a point. Some of them do like to live as the beggars live, and have no wish to go back to responsible lives now that there is no need for Invernairn to keep discreetly out of sight of the King's soldiers. I have sworn an oath to our new King, and I can now rebuild Invernairn, though it will be an irksome task,' he added, grimly. 'My household will not be rich, with soft living, for some time.'

'What about all the things you have begged?' asked Innes.

'I only begged what kept life and soul together,' said Ruari Stewart, with the glint back in his eyes. 'What else would my servants do? Till the land which the

King had taken? Ask for food at a poor cotter's door? Nay, we begged from those who could afford to share and earned them a place in Heaven.'

'And perhaps earned yourself a place in Hell,' said Innes, then she could have wished the words unsaid as the light faded a little from Ruari Stewart's eyes.

'You need a good husband to keep that sharp tongue in order, Mistress Innes, and that's just what you are going to get!'

She gasped as she began to realise the import of his words and her heart beat so wildly in her ribs that it must surely take wings. Already it seemed that it had taken wings! Ruari had gone to swear an oath of fealty so that he could walk proudly once more, and he was now going to take her for his lady. He must have arranged marriage at a nearby church. She glowed inwardly with the warmth of a flame which had been lit and which threatened to consume her whole body. She was going to belong to Ruari Stewart, and, even as the knowledge lit her heart, she knew she wanted no other fate.

But some queer perverse imp in her character longed to make sure that he knew she was no ripe plum to fall into his lap. He would have to try that little harder to win her.

'I begin to understand your meaning, sir,' she said with mock horror. 'Now that Invernairn has been returned to you, you would settle down with a wife. But would you take a wife whether she wishes to say yea or nay? What makes you suppose I should answer in the proper spirit when asked to make my vows before the priest?'

Ruari's face went white and he stood up abruptly.

'There is no need to have hysterics, Mistress,' he told her. 'I am no bridegroom for you. I have arranged a match such as your own brother could not have done better. The head of our house is Sir Alexander Stewart of Glenallyn, my own cousin, and recently he was widowed when the Lady Elspeth died when brought to child-bed. He has no son and no heir but for myself. He needs a good, strong wife to bear him fine sons, and you are as well formed as any he could find. He will have you, Mistress, and none shall look for a Frazer amongst the Stewarts. You will be able to sleep safe in your bed with Alexander to look after you. I can think of nowhere that would suit you so well.'

Innes' face had been scarlet, but now she was paper-white; although her body was still burning with inner fire, this time ashamedly. She had practically offered herself to Ruari Stewart, and he had turned her down in favour of his cousin . . . a widower! He, himself, did not care for her. He only wanted to be rid of her. And he would give her to a cousin whom he no doubt saw regularly so that she would have to entertain him when he came to Glenallyn. She would never be able to bear it.

'I will not,' she said, in a choked voice. 'I will not marry your cousin. He is a stranger to me. You cannot make me.'

'Your brother would turn you over and beat you,' said Ruari wearily. 'I will leave you to sleep on it. Like it or not, you leave for Glenallyn in the morning.'

He rose from his seat on the wooden settle near the window, and left the chamber, closing the heavy door. Innes tried to force back the tears, but soon they were streaming down her face and she was sobbing with shame and anger, and a queer empty ache in her heart. She felt humiliated beyond measure. Since coming to Invernairn, she had set herself up as being superior to women like Lizzie, and could not think other than that Ruari Stewart would hold her in respect because she was a lady born. They were equals, she had believed, and he must surely see how right and proper it was for them to marry. They had both lost their homes, but Ruari could now rebuild his openly and she still had sufficient assets to help him in this. Why, she had almost told him about Eleanor's strongbox which she had hidden under the bank of the stream. He might have taken her jewels, and still insisted on marrying her to his cousin! Oh, he was probably doing his best for her, but her heart ached that he preferred a servant girl to herself. She hated Ruari Stewart!

Innes sobbed until she was tired, then she dropped into an exhausted sleep; and when morning came, she awoke heavy-eyed when Lizzie brought her a plate of steaming gruel.

'Ye'll need this to warm ye on the journey,' she said, almost kindly.

'I do not want it,' said Innes.

'You will eat it,' said a stern voice from the doorway, 'every morsel. Your clothing will be packed and Lizzie will find you the best of your travelling gowns. I do not want my cousin to see a scarecrow arriving on his doorstep, or one fainting from lack of meat. You will eat everything Lizzie puts before you.'

'I do not have to obey you,' cried Innes, looking stonily at Ruari. 'You are not my guardian.'

'I can think of someone who may consider herself your guardian,' Ruari remarked, silkily.

Innes rubbed a hand over her weary eyes and looked at him, so that he came into the room.

'Come now, Mistress Innes, life has not dealt too badly with you,' he said, gently. 'Do not struggle so hard against the tide, and . . . ' his voice dropped as he turned away, ' . . . do not make it so hard on others.'

She stared at him sullenly. What others? Was he talking about Lizzie? Would he be ill-tempered enough to beat Lizzie if Innes refused to do her bidding?

'Very well, I shall eat it,' she said, 'but should I be ill on the journey, sir, I can only crave your indulgence.'

'You have my indulgence, Mistress Innes,' he said, very softly. 'You will have no cause to regret your own estate, I assure you. Lady Stewart of Glenallyn is no mean personage.'

She wanted to cry out, again, that she would have none of it but her tongue was stilled. Perhaps Sir Alexander would be a fair-minded man and would not force her to keep a bargain she had never made.

'I will take care of your purse,' Ruari said, picking it up again. 'It is but a small dowry, but it is something. You will not go to your bridegroom a pauper.'

She bit her lip. If he had offered for her, she would have been far from being a pauper! But now he would never know that he had had a substantial dowry within his grasp and had thrown it away. Now he would never know about the strongbox.

* * *

Glenallyn Castle lay to the north-west of Invernairn and was a day's ride away, so that Ruari gave orders that their party must leave at dawn. He was determined that the journey must be accomplished in one day, not two.

The henchmen who accompanied them, with a woman servant for Innes, were shabbily clad, but they looked clean and respectable. Work was proceeding at Invernairn, and soon the castle would be habitable enough to receive any nobleman going about the King's business.

Old Hannah and Lizzie had hovered near the courtyard to watch the party ride away, and Innes had already thanked them, then pressed a gold coin into their hands. Now that she was going, there was little cause for hatred or jealousy, and Innes felt too miserable to envy Lizzie any more. Her heart had soon grown bitter towards Ruari Stewart and anyone who wanted him, could have him, and welcome.

She was unused to such long hours in the saddle and soon her body ached with the weariness of the journey. The weather was now warmer and the days longer before sunset; so that, in spite of herself, she found enchantment in the distant purple mountains, the crystal clear streams and the copses of fresh green trees which afforded shelter from the sun.

Other travellers were abroad; noblemen with well-armed henchmen, packmen, holy men and poor people seeking employment. Innes surreptitiously parted with another gold piece as they passed a family who looked dull and enfeebled with starvation. She had slipped from her horse and pressed the coin into the woman's hand, and the joy on the thin face was a memory which stayed with her for some time.

Ruari rode up beside her after she remounted.

'Your money will not last long if you dole it out in this way,' he said. 'First of all to Hannah and Lizzie, who have no need of it, and now to those poor wretches who had little use for it either.'

'They should have been given much more,' cried Innes. 'They are starving.'

'It will be thought that they stole it.'

'Oh!' cried Innes. 'I cannot believe it

. . . not if she spends wisely.'

'She will be eating wisely ere now,' said Ruari. 'We shared out some of our meat. But have a thought, Mistress, and if anything troubles you, then ask advice. Ignorance can do more harm than good.'

Innes bit her lip. She had wanted to hate him, but now she could see that he was worthy of her admiration. He was used to taking care of people and to feeding those who needed to be fed, and now he was beginning to accomplish much through honest toil, having sampled the degradation of beggary.

The sun was sinking behind the mountains and the sky had been painted every hue from deepest red to palest silvery-pink as it slowly sank to its nadir. The glowing colours formed a backcloth for Glenallyn Castle as they rode into the courtyard, and in spite of herself, Innes could only gaze around the beautiful castle with silent admiration. There was a curtain on three sides, the fourth being bounded by a river, and Innes was struck by the way the castle had been kept. The courtyard had been swept and brushed clean for their arrival, and servants had come out to greet them and to help them from the saddle.

Innes was too tired to view the place in any great detail; but she was conscious of warmth of welcome, of long corridors and many apartments, of the great hall where a fire burned in spite of the warmer day, and of richly-furnished bedrooms to which they were conducted. She had received the briefest glimpse of Sir Alexander Stewart, a tall thin dark man to whom she made a brief curtsey; then she was helped along to the room where two maidservants soon unbuttoned her out of her soiled travelling clothes and into a bath of scented water, provided for her toilet.

The warm water was relaxing and cleansed her mind as well as her body. She was all but asleep when the linen bedgown was dropped over her head and she was helped into bed. The maidservants had been quietly deferential and the woman who had ridden from Invernairn in attendance had been taken to the servants' quarters in the west wing near to the large kitchens.

Innes had a moment of panic when she thought about what the morrow might bring, but her bones still ached in spite of the warm bath, and she drifted into sleep.

She dreamed of Ruari Stewart whose dark handsome face was turned to her mockingly, occasionally allowing her to glimpse the shadowy figure who stood behind him, his cousin Alexander. Yet every time she tried to catch a glimpse of Alexander, Ruari stood in the way.

'I cannot marry him. I do not love him,' she repeated and found that the words were on her lips as she awoke to a bright chamber, full of sunshine.

It seemed as though she had slept late and she sat up quickly in the warm comfortable bed which smelled of clean fresh drapes, richly embroidered by a sempstress of talent. The room was the most luxurious Innes had ever seen, with soft skins on the floor to give warmth to her feet and brightly polished chests and cabinets with pretty carvings for decoration.

A woman servant hurried in, exclaiming with alarm when she saw Innes standing on the floor, clad only in her bedgown.

'A wind can blaw cauld from the mountains,' she said, 'even if the sun is up. You will need your clothing, my lady. Master Stewart said to put a braw dress on you and he would come and escort you to Sir Alexander . . . Glenallyn, himself, as you know.'

She did not know, thought Innes, but she was not going to question the servants, or hint that she knew nothing about Glenallyn. Sir Alexander, and Ruari, must be kinsmen of the Royal Household, even though it was a few generations back, and Glenallyn might have been built when the relationship was closer. She would have enjoyed

questioning Ruari in other circumstances, but she would have little
chance to get to know Glenallyn. She
would not stay here for very long
without fulfilling her obligations to Sir
Alexander, and she had no intention of
doing that.

The maidservant brought her a tray
of food for breakfast, and there was
even a small piece of bread such as she
had not tasted since Eleanor had served
it up at her table. Innes ate it with relish
and after a leisurely toilet, when the
maidservant expertly combed out her
dark red hair and put a circlet of velvet
on top of her head, she felt ready for
anything . . . almost. The good plain
food and fresh air had been doing
wonders for her in recent weeks and she
knew that her body had grown tall and
strong, yet lissom and graceful, as her
breasts became well-formed and her
waist trimmed to neatness.

The lovely fur-trimmed gown which
she again wore was very becoming, and
the maidservant was almost overcome

in her admiration.

'You look like a princess, my lady,' she said, shyly. 'Your hair shines like dark copper.'

'I was glad to have the dust removed,' said Innes. 'It was a long ride from Invernairn.' She paused. 'I would like to see Glenallyn in the light of day, and to see the kitchens. One can always tell a great deal about a dwelling just by looking at the kitchens.'

'Oh no, my lady!' The maidservant looked at her with horror. 'Sir Alexander will take you round. You must not look at the servants until the master takes you round. Lady Elspeth always walked round the kitchens, but everyone knew the proper time. Everything must always be done at the proper time.'

Innes said no more. She sensed that the castle was well run. Had Lady Elspeth set the scene while she was mistress, and it had all just proceeded on oiled wheels, or was it Sir Alexander who liked good order? Perhaps he was an exacting man.

Innes had to sit in her chamber whilst the hours drifted past before Ruari Stewart eventually came to find her. By then she was torn between relief that her sojourn was over and anger that it had lasted so long.

'Ah, Mistress Innes!' he greeted her, 'our business has taken longer than we expected, my cousin and I, but be pleased to come now and make the acquaintance of Sir Alexander.'

'I see that he is as eager to seek my company as I am to seek his,' said Innes, tartly, so that Ruari turned and gave her his amused grin. She stared back at him defiantly, and saw the measuring look deepen in his eyes.

'For the love of God, look to your tongue,' he said in a low voice. 'I do my best for you, but you act as though you are one of the princesses.'

Innes bit her lip. The maidservant had said she looked like a princess. Perhaps, in the distress of her situation, she was giving herself airs and graces she had never possessed by way of reassurance.

'I . . . I am sorry,' she whispered, and he turned to lead her along a labyrinth of corridors to the great hall where a log fire had been laid but not lit. Innes had expected that there might be a few people gathered together, since Glenallyn appeared to be full of activity; but Sir Alexander Stewart was alone in the great hall but for an elderly woman who was, apparently, acting as housekeeper.

'Leave us now, Marjorie,' he was saying. 'We will be at our meat presently. Delay the food until we are ready.'

'Very good, Sir Alexander,' she said, formally.

Ruari put a hand under Innes' elbow and drew her forward.

'Here is the lady I told you about, Cousin,' he said. 'Mistress Innes Frazer, this is Sir Alexander Stewart . . . Mistress Frazer, Alexander.'

Innes dropped a small curtsey and

Sir Alexander acknowledged her presence with a bow.

'I have met your father, Mistress Frazer,' he said, 'a few years ago, and your brother, Archibald. He and Graham were friends and my own kinsman, Sir Robert Stewart, though he had no support from me.'

Innes blushed. She could see that Sir Alexander had only contempt for her brother's part in the murder of King James.

'I'm sure Mistress Innes would agree with you, Cousin,' Ruari was saying, smoothly. 'She did not always agree with the sentiments of her step-brother.'

'Aye, that is so. He was against the King through his mother's family.'

He stared for a long time at Innes who gazed back, frankly. Sir Alexander was probably ten years older than Ruari and was, perhaps, in his late thirties. He was not an old man but he looked settled in his ways. His dark hair was growing sparse, and, on closer inspection, was liberally sprinkled with grey.

He had the same dark eyes as Ruari, but where Ruari's could brighten to devilment and laughter, Sir Alexander's were as cold as pebbles.

'And now my Cousin Ruari has made himself responsible for you, Mistress Frazer,' he said, deliberately, 'since you were left without friends after the Queen had taken her revenge. Oh, I believe she went demented with grief over the King's murder and extracted a terrible revenge. She never rested until the last of the men who had conspired against the King were tortured and punished. Graham suffered most of all, but he still maintained that James was a tyrant king.'

Innes shivered and Ruari knelt down and blew the log fire into life. There was sea coal in a box and he threw on a few pieces.

'Mistress Innes is cold,' he explained briefly, and Alexander merely bowed in acknowledgment.

'The Queen might pardon you, since you were only slightly connected to the affair, but she might still be in her mood of hate and revenge. It was fortunate that Cousin Ruari was so well acquainted with your family and managed to hide you until the worst of the storm was past.'

Innes threw a startled look at Ruari. For once he looked disconcerted, and it occurred to her that his cousin knew nothing of his begging activities. He met her eyes and after a long anxious moment during which she held her tongue, she could see the smile lighting up his eyes once more, and her heart leapt with love for him. He was twice as big a man as his cousin, but it seemed that he was still bent on handing her over to Glenallyn.

Remembrance brought a flush to her cheeks again.

'We will not beat about the bush,' Alexander was saying. 'I have gone into your family connections, Mistress Frazer, and I know you have lost your possessions through no fault of your own, so I shall not expect a dowry.

Glenallyn is rich enough already . . . '

He paused as the elderly woman, Marjorie, suddenly bustled in.

'Yer meat will be burned to a cinder, Master Alexander, if it keeps much longer and you need your nourishment like I've always told you.'

'And you know what I have told you, old woman,' growled Alexander.

'The servants are without their meat,' she said, stubbornly. 'Ye stop them as well as yourself.'

'Oh, serve it up and we will sup now.'

He conducted Innes and Ruari to a long table, well appointed, with bowls of fruit and sweet spices.

'Marjorie was my nurse when I was a bairn,' he said to Innes. 'She forgets she is not my mother.'

For once the cold dark eyes were warm, but the faint smile on his face did nothing to endear him to Innes. She had tried to look appealingly to Ruari but he was now completely aloof from any discussion and returned her gaze coldly. It seemed as though he had found her an unwanted responsibility. Innes being the daughter of a nobleman, he had hesitated to use her as he used Lizzie, and had not known otherwise what to do with her. Now he was handing her on to Alexander, who surely did not need a wife when he had the competent Marjorie to run Glenallyn for him.

But . . . of course! . . . she had forgotten. Alexander had no son and she . . . she was a strong young woman of good stock. She was to be a breeding mare. But Glenallyn could choose practically any young woman in the kingdom. Why should he offer for her? Ruari had used some persuasion, thought Innes. He must want to be rid of her badly.

She had no appetite for the food which was placed in front of her. It was as dainty as any which Eleanor had served and more appetizing than anything she had eaten at Invernairn, but she was conscious that, after the dinner was eaten, she would have to find an answer for Sir Alexander as to why she was refusing him. Such a refusal would be unheard of, and if her brother had arranged it, she would have been beaten and starved into submission.

But she would rather work as a servant and keep her freedom than give herself to this cold man. Ruari looked equally cold, but she knew there could be fire in him. Alexander made her shiver as his eyes ran over her. She knew there would be little love in her life if she married him and she could not live without love.

Alexander also ate sparingly, but his wine glass was replenished a few times with disapproving noises from Marjorie. Ruari had grown sullen, and once or twice Innes had caught him staring at her beneath his brows, though his eyes dropped when her own challenged him.

Finally Alexander rose, slightly unsteadily, and escorted Innes back to a seat by the fireside, bidding the servants clear away the food after they had eaten their fill.

'Yer're a healthy young woman and ready to be wed,' said Alexander without preamble. 'We will have the priest perform the ceremony. We have our own chapel at Glenallyn such as not many nobles have.'

'But . . . but . . . ' Innes felt trapped. 'You risk the Queen's anger, sir,' she cried.

'The Queen will not meddle with Glenallyn,' said Alexander, icily. 'Do you not know that we are in friendship to Douglas? Sir William Crichton . . . Crichton is looking after the boy King at Edinburgh, but Livingstone would fain get his claws on him. They are like twa dogs over a bone. I tell you Scotland will be ill-governed now that the great, powerful James has gone and it is the nobles who will have the power. The Queen will not offend the nobles. She might need their protection.'

There was silence whilst Alexander stared at Innes moodily.

'We will perform the marriage before

my cousin returns to Invernairn. He can be witness.'

'I do not consent,' said Innes, her heart beginning to beat loudly.

There was a heavy, stunned silence as Ruari sat up in his chair whilst Alexander remained almost motionless.

'What is this?' he asked after a moment. 'Am I expected to woo a young female of no substance? Mistress Frazer has a fine body, Cousin Ruari, but you did not mention that her intelligence was at fault. I have no time for preliminaries, Mistress, nor would I know how to woo thee. I do not know any pretty words, like the late King, nor can I play the lute.'

'Sir, I would marry for love,' said Innes, almost desperately.

'Love!' Alexander's lips curled. 'I married the Lady Elspeth for love but she was as delicate as ... as a moonbeam, like others of her stamp. She could not bear my son.'

For a brief moment Innes caught sight of the grief which still lay on the heart of this cold man, but which he kept well covered. She would never be able to reach his heart to dispel the grief nor did she want to. She had a glimpse of the loneliness which lay ahead for her if she consented to the marriage, and her back stiffened. She could learn to love Glenallyn, but she would also grow dull with weariness and boredom, even if she bore a dozen children. They would be Sir Alexander's children as well as her own and the thought revolted her. She looked with distaste at his thinning hair and slack mouth, and the eyes which were heavy with drink. The more she saw of him, the less he attracted her.

Ruari had been very silent but now he turned to her, sternly.

'I hope you know what you are about, Mistress Innes,' he said, heavily. 'You must know I cannot return you to Invernairn. There . . . there are reasons . . . '

'Lizzie.'

He stared at her. 'I do not understand you, Mistress.'

Her lips curled. 'How can you not?'

'She would not dare to inform on you, Mistress, but if you stay here, you will be safe. You will be a lady of position and substance.'

Alexander was looking at her sourly. The wine had upset his stomach, and the nagging pain which troubled him from time to time was beginning to gnaw at his innards and upset his temper.

'I do not intend to plead with . . . with a child who is nobody . . . to be the lady of Glenallyn,' he said, almost snarling with anger. In truth he had been pleased with the young female his cousin had found for him. She was well formed and graceful and would have borne him sweet children, but she had insulted him by turning down his offer.

'Since Mistress Frazer refuses marriage, she cannot stay at Glenallyn either,' he told Ruari. 'You had better go to your room, Mistress, whilst my cousin and I make arrangements for you. Since you are so haughty you may have cause to regret it. The new arrangements may not be to your liking. I will send for you when we know whither to conduct you.'

'Very well, sir,' said Innes, dropping a curtsey.

Sir Alexander had called a maidservant to conduct her to her room and Innes followed her, her head held high so that she should not reveal the fear which was suddenly growing in her. Ruari Stewart had been her captor and protector, since she had lost her family, but now he was going out of her life. She had also spurned Sir Alexander because . . . because he was not Ruari, said her heart. But now she might be going to something a great deal less attractive. Where would they send her, and what would she be required to do? Perhaps, very soon, she would be regretting that she had refused Sir Alexander. Nor would she get another chance. She had seen the look on his face, of anger and humiliation that she dared to refuse him. It had been inflamed with wine, but it would be just as strong when morning came.

The maidservant scarcely spoke to her, and Innes wondered if already the servants throughout the castle knew that their Lord had been refused. It would spread like wildfire. Now she would be treated with reserve. She was not going to be the mistress of Glenallyn.

★　★　★

It was like being in prison, thought Innes, even though her accommodation was fresh and comfortable. The weather had warmed after a very cold winter, but the thick stone walls of the castle kept the interior chilly.

Innes asked if the housekeeper would see her and when the stern elderly woman arrived bristling, no doubt expecting a complaint, Innes merely asked if there was mending to be done.

'It is done by our sewing woman, Mistress,' the woman told her, rather sourly, 'in the sewing room.'

'But surely there must be something which you might not find time to do, such as Lady Sarah would have done.'

The housekeeper's face darkened.

'That is for the master to say,' she replied, tight-lipped. Her look said that Innes must be very conceited to have refused such a man as Sir Alexander Frazer.

'I find that time is heavy on my hands,' said Innes, determined to make one last appeal.

'The master left no instructions,' the woman told her.

'Then he has ridden out?' asked Innes. 'Perhaps I could see Master Stewart.'

'Master Stewart has been recalled to Invernairn,' the woman said with ill-concealed satisfaction, 'but he returns . . . ' she stopped, biting her lip, ' . . . shortly.'

So they had gone away and left her!

'I would like to walk in the

courtyard,' she said.

'You are to keep to your chamber.'

'Oh, please,' said Innes and perhaps something about her youth caught the older woman's heart, and she hesitated.

'Perhaps the maidservant can walk with me and a henchman as a guard, but I have no plans to run away. Where would I go?' she asked.

'Aye . . . well, then, Mistress . . . '

The older woman nodded her head gravely. 'If you make it a short wee while, Mistress, and come back to this apartment before the Master returns.'

'That I can promise you,' said Innes rather wearily.

The young maidservant, Sarah Laidlaw, accompanied Innes silently as she was conducted once again to the great hall, and then to the ground floor, which was mainly given over to store rooms.

Innes was conducted to the courtyard where she wandered around in the sunshine while servants went about their duties, attending to the horses and cleaning up the courtyard. Innes could see that they were working quite well, but she could understand now why Sir Alexander was in need of a wife. Now that she was close to the rooms in daylight she could see that some things were being neglected which a lady would notice and put right. Marjorie would not have the same obedience from the other servants that the mistress of the castle would expect.

'Will you show me over Glenallyn?' she asked, turning again to Sarah Laidlaw.

The girl grew alarmed.

'Oh, Mistress, I durst not. The master asked that you should be kept to your room. He rode out after Master Stewart.'

'It is so dull doing nothing, Sarah,' Innes coaxed. 'See . . . there is the main entrance, surely, where we entered the castle when I first came. We will go in there and if Sir Alexander should return, I shall go quickly back to my room.'

Sarah looked relieved and accompanied Innes with alacrity. They walked into a guardroom where a few armed men were apparently on duty, and again entered the great hall, where Innes walked determinedly towards the north wing.

'Oh, Mistress, you cannot go there,' Sarah objected. 'That . . . there are the kitchens.'

'I should like to see the kitchens,' said Innes. She could not go back to the boredom of her room!

There was much giggling as she walked in and a great deal of confusion amongst the kitchen maids who seemed to be spending more time enjoying honey cake than cleaning up the mess. The fireplace was huge but there were three windows nearby to allow the air to blow fresh. Innes looked pointedly at the floor which was not as clean as she would have wished, and the stone sink was also greasy and the drain malodorous.

Innes had no authority to send the

maidservants about their business, but she looked at everything carefully and saw one or two women beginning to scrub the long heavy tables.

'It seems that there is much to be done,' she remarked to Sarah. 'Parts of Glenallyn are kept clean and fresh, but equally important places are neglected.'

'It will be done before the next wolf hunt,' the girl said. 'Sir Alexander entertains well after a wolf hunt and likes the rushes to be changed.'

'I am happy to hear that,' said Innes.

She had walked further along the north wing and saw that it also housed a dungeon, the sight of which made her shudder.

The south wing was given over to private apartments, which included the room she had been given, and she had no wish to peep and pry into the others. The guardrobe had a flue leading to containers which, Sarah assured her, were emptied daily.

'The master beat Will Meikle because he forgot and the well almost became 'contaminated,' Sarah confided.

'Does the master often beat his servants?' Innes asked, casually, and heard the girl's small intake of breath.

'Not often . . . sometimes,' she whispered. 'They deserve it,' she assured Innes. 'If we do nothing wrong, he does not beat us.'

Again Innes nodded. Perhaps Sir Alexander was no better, or worse, than noblemen in his position, and she had longed to box the ears of the lazy kitchen maids herself.

Near the great hall, where Sir Alexander no doubt entertained many guests, was a tiny chapel. It was hardly more than a recess, and Innes shivered as the cold of it bit into her bones. This was where she would have been married to Sir Alexander, if she had consented.

'I will go back to my chamber now,' she told Sarah, who looked relieved. The girl had softened towards her and had given her small snippets of information, but she was obviously glad to be free of the responsibility of keeping an eye on her.

Innes sat down on a bench near the window and rested her head for a moment. The chapel had reminded her that her situation was greatly lacking in security. Perhaps she should have knelt and offered a prayer for courage to face whatever was coming to her. She could not go back to Invernairn and she could not stay at Glenallyn. And by now Dundallon would be in the hands of the soldiers.

So where could she go?

5

'Edinburgh! Edinburgh Castle! Into the Queen's household!' cried Innes. 'Oh, sir . . . surely you must know that I cannot!'

'It seems that there is a great deal that you cannot do, Mistress Frazer,' said Sir Alexander, coldly. 'Since you cannot become my wife, there are very few arrangements which can be made for a young female of your background. I gave the matter great thought, and I decided to see the Queen, who is in need of a nursemaid for her daughters . . . sisters to our young King James II. She believes you to be Mistress Jane Innes, a young kinswoman of mine, who has recently been orphaned, and she is willing to try your services.'

'But, the Queen . . . '

'Is your enemy, or your brother's . . . late brother's. But it is my experience that one rarely notices what is under one's nose. If she learns of your existence at all, Mistress, she is unlikely to look for you in her own household.'

Innes was silent, feeling almost too frightened to speak. Sir Alexander was extracting a fine revenge for her insult to him.

'Does Ruari agree to this?' she asked in a whisper.

'Master Stewart has been recalled to Invernairn on important business,' Alexander told her very coldly. 'I do not think he had a great deal of time to be anxious on your account. He has much to do to deal with his own affairs. Swearing loyalty to the new King means that he must take his place, now, in his country's affairs, and can deal only with important matters as they arise. He must tread carefully and prove himself.'

Innes felt her eyes stinging with tears. She was of no importance to Ruari. He was Sir Alexander's heir and the thought had teased at her for some time. Surely it was not in Ruari's interest to wed her to Sir Alexander, and to hope that sons would be born to them. Then it had struck her that Ruari had preferred to see her son inherit Glenallyn rather than marry her himself. The thought had been even more humiliating, and she felt anger stirring in her again.

But now someone else would be the mother of the future heir to Glenallyn. And she . . . she would be living a life of terror where every day she would be poised on a razor's edge. At any moment she might give herself away to Queen Johanna that she was the sister of one of the men who had murdered the King.

'I would ask you to reconsider, sir,' she said to Sir Alexander, 'and find me a situation in your household. I . . . I saw the kitchens yesterday and . . . and some of the other chambers, and, truly, they are in need of a woman's touch.'

'I gave orders that you were to stay in your room,' he thundered. 'I shall have the hide of the one who has disobeyed me.'

'It was not the fault of a servant,' she cried. 'I . . . I found my way there by myself.'

She could now see the naked cruelty in him and she was glad she had refused him. How well did Ruari Stewart know his cousin when he could hand her over to his care? Perhaps they were both alike, deep down. It must be so when they could play such a cruel trick, and find her a place in the Queen's service. Was Ruari a party to that?

'I have no time for shilly-shallying,' Sir Alexander said, turning away abruptly. 'You must know it is not seemly for a young female of your years to be in my service, or my cousin's for that matter, when we are not truly kin. And do you think it pleases me that you would be a servant in my household, yet disdain to be its mistress? Am I such a monster? Well, no matter, since I would not have you now at any price. I will tolerate no insults from a young female in your position.

'Pack what you wish to take and be ready to leave within the hour. I will conduct you to Edinburgh myself, since I have claimed you as a kinswoman; after which I wish to hear no more from you. You will need an escort because these are troubled times to be abroad, and because my cousin made himself responsible for you in honour to your family. I will respect that honour. You will be some six or seven hours in the saddle, so see that your clothing is suitable.'

Innes lifted her head proudly. She wished she could tell him that he need not concern himself about her, nor need Master Stewart, but she knew herself to be helpless.

'I will be ready, sir,' she said, huskily.

★ ★ ★

The small township of Edinburgh lay to the east and the winds began to grow cooler as they rode towards the eastern half of the country. In spite of her apprehension, Innes found that the ride in the brisk air, refreshing after Glenallyn, was invigorating and she found much to interest her. They were riding towards more fertile land and she was interested to see small farmsteads and turf cottages such as were common around Dundallon.

The King had been murdered at Perth and, as Sir Alexander had explained, the Queen had been afraid to remain there, so she had come to Edinburgh with the new King to be with Sir William Crichton, who had been friend to her late husband.

Archibald had often talked about Edinburgh Castle, which was a fine stronghold, even though it had been captured by Edward the First of England after a siege lasting ten days. But that was a long time ago, thought Innes . . . almost 150 years, when the brave Robert the Bruce recaptured it for Scotland.

The castle of Edinburgh could be seen for some distance, built high up on a rock, a great fortress for the new King; though Innes felt a coldness lying on her heart at the sight of it, and a sense of foreboding. It was like a prison to her, and her heart was heavy and sick with dread as they rode up the incline to the main entrance, where Sir Alexander had to satisfy the guard as to his credentials.

Inside the courtyard there were scenes of great activity, and Innes watched with fascination after their horses had been led away and servants seemed to scurry here and there, busy with the life of the fine castle which housed their King.

Sir Alexander had gone to report to the Master of the Household that his young kinswoman had arrived to take up her duties as one of the nursemaids to the young princesses. For a long time Innes waited with dread to be conducted to the Queen; then she was led to a small chamber which she would share with a number of other women, cramped though it was, and her clothing was laid out on a chest.

After refreshing herself with a wash and change of clothing, her garments being very soiled from the journey, she was led to the great hall where a meal had been provided. Sir Alexander and other barons had already gathered, and Innes was placed amongst the servants, but she was too hungry to do more than eat the meat which was placed before her. The Queen and the princesses were in their own quarters, she learned, and she would not see them until the following morning.

* * *

When Sir Archibald had been entertaining friends, Innes had often listened to the gossip of the ladies whose prime topic of conversation was the Royal household.

King James the First had been captured by the English when he was a boy of fourteen, and held to ransom, but when his father Robert III heard of his son's capture he collapsed and died. James' uncle, the Duke of Albany, became Regent and the ransom was not paid.

'The English held on to James for eighteen years,' Archibald had once said to Eleanor. 'They were brave to have put up with him for so long.'

'He should have been returned to us to take his rightful place on the throne,' said Eleanor.

'At a cost of £40,000?' asked Archibald, 'for expenses for educating him and keeping him!'

'Most of it still to be paid,' Eleanor pointed out. 'At least he got that out of his capture . . . a fine education and a beautiful wife. Those who have seen Queen Johanna say she is most beautiful, and the King calls her his milk-white dove.'

'Oh, she is well enough,' said Archibald, carelessly.

His mother's people had supported

the King's uncle and King James had proved to have a long memory. The Duke of Albany's son, Duke Murdoch, had paid the penalty for his father's procrastination in paying ransom for the King, as had others who had sided with him.

But Eleanor's own people had always been loyal to the rightful King, as had Innes' mother's people; and perhaps there had been a delight, only understood by a woman, in the romance between James and the Lady Joan Beaufort. The King was a poet and the poetry he wrote for his lady tore at the heart. Most women in the kingdom would like to be loved as the King had loved his Queen. Yet it was as a result of that fierce, burning love that her own people had been destroyed, thought Innes. Some said the Queen had not been in her right mind because of grief, and that the tortures suffered by those who were guilty of his murder were the most terrible ever practised on human beings. Innes felt sick when she remembered some of the tales the beggars had whispered to one another. Even the most hardened of them had been horrified.

As she waited to be taken to the Queen, Innes' heart felt cold with dread. She thought about Invernairn and Lizzie, in her beggar's clothes, seemed a warm human being with whom she could talk. Here she was a stranger, and although one or two women had spoken to her and tried to make her welcome, she could not tell them the truth of her situation. She was Jane Innes, kinswoman to Sir Alexander Stewart, who had been engaged to be of service to the princesses, one of whom was being sent, as a bride, to the French court.

The Earl of Douglas was acting as Regent, but the care and education of the boy King was in the hands of Sir William Crichton. Innes was curious, too, about the small boy who was their new King and she had asked Alexander about him. However, Alexander had been in no mood to hold conversation with her and had merely remarked that he had a fiery red mark on his face.

Alexander had left for Glenallyn that morning, saying that there was to be a wapinshaw on the following day; and he would have to arrange for his men to show their weapons to the King's officers, according to their stations, and to demonstrate their powers in using those weapons. Sometimes his tenants had grown slack in not using their weapons and practising shooting their arrows at a target near the Church, so that they were useless as archers if the time came when they were required to fight for their lord. Alexander had fined the indolent men a sheep, but some of the younger men had been caught playing football, against the law, and had been fined accordingly. Most of them preferred to fight with pikes in any case, or even axes, as Alexander explained, grumbling to Innes, or perhaps grumbling aloud to himself as they rode along.

Now that he had gone, Innes could even have wished for his return. She had never felt more lonely or frightened in her life. After the rape of Dundallon she had been too numbed to be afraid; and, even at their most terrible, the Invernairn beggars had had a warmth of spirit which was curiously lacking in Edinburgh. It was as though passions and anger had raged so strongly that emotion had now drained away in its aftermath. Servants still scurried here and there, going about their duties, but there was a curious undercurrent of fear which chilled the heart. Memories of cruelty and torture were still very fresh and Innes knew that she was not the only one who felt afraid. Fear lay in the future as well as the past.

Finally, a servant came and asked Innes to follow him to the Queen's presence.

The Royal apartments were warm and stuffy, on a mild day, and the little princesses played happily around the room as Innes walked forward with shaking knees. The Queen was keeping her children round her like a mother hen.

Innes curtseyed deeply, then she was looking into the cold dead eyes of Queen Johanna. She was only conscious of the other woman's deep suffering, and somehow her own fears were held at bay as the Queen spoke to her.

'Sir Alexander Stewart's kinswoman, Mistress Jane Innes, connected on your mother's side, Mistress Innes. How old are you, child?'

'Seventeen, y-your Majesty,' Innes stammered.

'Are you strong?'

'Yes, ma'am.'

'Healthy?'

'Yes, ma'am.'

'I will have the physician check your health. The Royal children must not be exposed to infection. You look a fine strong girl, and your family are well enough, since Sir Alexander has vouched for you and he is loyal. We cannot always depend on loyalty these days.'

Innes said nothing but her heart quaked. Inwardly she was grateful to Alexander who had put his own reputation at risk when he vouched for her. Then she remembered Alexander's scathing remarks about the power being now in the hands of the barons and how none would dare touch Stewart of Glenallyn. Alexander would have vouched for her carelessly, out of arrogance, and certainly not out of regard for her.

'Are you used to children?' the Queen was asking. 'How many are in your family?'

'I . . . I am alone, ma'am,' said Innes, huskily, 'but I was used to my brother's . . . brother's children,' she ended, almost biting her tongue while her heart thundered in her breast. How easy it was to make a mistake!

'Your brother? Where is your brother? Is he responsible for you, and not Sir Alexander?'

'I . . . ' Innes was tongue-tied. 'M-my brother is dead,' she whispered, her eyes wide with fright. So it had all been for nothing. In another moment the Queen would ask the question which would reveal her true identity and she was stiff with fear as the royal lady stared hard at her.

'Are you afraid of me, child?' she asked.

Innes had grown almost faint with fear and she ran her tongue over her lips.

'Yes, ma'am,' she whispered, again.

Queen Johanna rubbed a hand over her forehead.

'So much hate,' she said, wearily, 'so much revenge. How can one fight evil, but with more evil and banish love with fear? I am feared where once I was loved. Now I live in fear . . . for my son . . . for the King . . . '

Innes stood very still, knowing that the Queen was talking more to herself than to her. She saw that the royal lady's beautiful hair was sprinkled with silver and there were lines at the side of her mouth which betrayed the tension in her; but she could also see the purity of her face and she could well understand how beautiful the Queen must have looked when she was young and happy.

'You will see my lady Gordon, who will explain your duties, Mistress Innes.' Suddenly the Queen smiled. 'Mistress Jane,' she corrected. 'You are little more than a child yourself. I shall go into your family background at a later date and you shall tell me about your life in your brother's home. I am interested in my people . . . the King's subjects. Archibald . . . the Earl of Douglas . . . is Regent . . . ' Her eyes grew rather blank again. 'He is not strong enough to hold such power, the power the Earl of Douglas should hold in the country. There will be no peace . . . ' Again her voice trailed off and again the Queen sat silent for a while.

'You will help the other women who serve us. See Lady Margaret . . . Lady

Gordon . . . ' she continued absently and Innes curtseyed and left the chamber.

Lady Margaret Gordon was a stout, elderly woman whose husband had been killed in the King's service. Her son had inherited the estate and Lady Margaret had come to join the Queen's household.

'Another Jane,' she said, looking closely at Innes. 'Aye . . . well . . . ye can take Jane Livingstone's place. She has been wedded to Sir Gavin Keith. He's maybe a wheen o' years too old for her, but he is weel enough to make a proper wife o' her, and he serves Douglas.'

Innes nodded and again her heart beat uncomfortably. She had met Sir Gavin Keith, whose land had adjoined Dundallon. He was old, with a bald head and three chins. She did not envy the new Lady Keith. But was her own situation so much better? Would it have been so very terrible to marry Alexander?

'Yes,' said her heart. No man was going to touch her but for love, and that had been thrown away. She drew a deep breath and followed Lady Gordon to a tiny chamber where she changed her clothing for a shapeless grey linen garment, and a cap to cover her hair.

'The older princesses are still sad and bewildered at losing their father,' Lady Gordon said. 'Be easy, Mistress Jane, though the Queen will not have them checked and they grow spoiled. Poor lady. She is in a dwam yet. You can help to feed the young ones and play with them, but not out of doors unless they are guarded by the soldiers. The Queen is feared and who can blame her, poor lady? Sir William Crichton is a good friend to her, but . . . well . . . there is nothing for you to worry about, child. Only you must be ever vigilant of the princesses and never take on the responsibility of looking after them on your own. A maidservant will always accompany you, and there will always be the soldiers on guard. And mind what I tell you, Mistress Jane.'

'Aye, my lady.'

'Good child. You are well enough brought up, I can see. Where do you belong to?'

'My . . . my parents are dead,' said Innes, forcing herself to speak bravely, 'but my kinsman, Sir Alexander Stewart, brought me here to the Queen's service.'

'Mind ye serve her well then, or it will not hold to the credit of your kinsman.'

'Aye, my lady,' said Innes, bobbing a curtsey.

The motherly woman's face crinkled.

'I like ye better than Livingstone,' she said. 'I think she told tales to her kinsman.'

'Her kinsman?'

'Sir Alexander Livingstone, Governor of Stirling. The Livingstones . . . they like power . . . '

Lady Margaret looked reflective, just as the Queen had done.

'Do your duty, child, but if you are

anxious about anything ye see, or hear, come and tell me. It is hard to tell friend from foe these days. There were friends of the King who turned into foes and foes who now claim to be friends of the new King, poor wee laddie.'

'Is he with the princesses, ma'am?' asked Innes.

'Bless you, no. He has to have his lessons and he is well looked after by Sir William. He had a fine crowning at Holyrood, though it should have been Scone. That it should.'

'I have heard that he has a red mark on his face,' said Innes.

'It does not mar his beauty,' said Lady Margaret, sharply. 'He is a fine wee man. I canna think of him as my liege lord, since he seems like my very own bairn, but he is every inch a king. He knows what is expected of him. Are ye promised to any man?'

Lady Margaret had gone off at a tangent and it was a moment before Innes could grasp the meaning of the question. When she did, her cheeks coloured rosily.

'No . . . no, ma'am,' she cried.

'No, but somebody has caught your fancy. Who is it?'

'No one, ma'am,' cried Innes.

She had a momentary glimpse of Ruari's dark face with his laughing eyes behind his beggar's disguise.

'No one who cares about me,' she said, almost bitterly.

'Very good, child. You will not be moon-gazing then. You will eat with the servants in the great hall. I will show you where. You will not sup at the same time as the other nursemaids. The princesses must not be left unattended. Edinburgh Castle is the most important castle in the land while the King resides here, and great barons come and go. See that your are not disrespectful to strangers. They are on lawful business, else they would not be allowed within the gates. But see, also, that you do not make up to them or the soldiers. I will have none o' that . . . ye understand?'

'Aye, my lady,' said Innes, wondering how she could remember all her instructions even if some would be easy to follow. She met the other nurse-maids, and wondered if she would ever be happy and settled in this great castle, where she could look down on the small township, then outwards towards the Waters of Leith. It was all so very strange and every bit as frightening as Invernairn had been when she first arrived there.

As she slept on her hard straw mattress, her weariness was so great that she had not been able to stay awake. Yet her last thought was for Ruari. Was he a foe, turned friend, to James II, such as Lady Gordon had mentioned? Would he be looked upon with suspicion? And if she betrayed herself, would the Queen's vengeance reach out to Sir Alexander . . . and to Ruari? Innes shivered and said a prayer to enable her to strengthen her spirit.

Yet in spite of everything, Innes felt keyed up and alive. Edinburgh was dangerous, but it was also exciting.

6

Innes soon became used to her duties as an assistant nursemaid to the royal children. The other nursemaids teased her because she was very quiet about her personal affairs, and believed this to be because of extreme shyness and awe of the Queen. One of the other nursemaids, Anna Gourlay, whose cot was next to her own, treated her with robust kindness and said she was unlikely to have cause to fear the Queen if she 'kept her nose clean'.

'She is recovering from her grief and shock, Jane,' she told Innes, 'and she was always a kind and gentle lady until our good King James was killed. I was at Blackfriars when it happened, you know.'

'Oh.' Innes hardly knew what to say, but Anna's eyes were round with the drama of the great tragedy which the people were beginning to resent. The removal of King James had left a vacuum which was proving dangerous for the country.

'Aye,' said Anna. 'The King was with the ladies and all was quiet, then we heard the soldiers coming along the corridor and looking in every room. Sir Robert Stewart, who looked after the household at Blackfriars, was a traitor and caused the locks to be spoiled, but Lady Catherine Douglas ran forward and thrust her arm through the bolt. We put the King down into a vault, and Her Majesty threw a rug over the trap-door and the ladies stood on the rug. The King might have escaped had he not blocked up the hole at the other end of the tunnel so that his tennis balls were not lost down the hole.'

Innes listened, her face very white as she thought of her brother's part in all this.

'Sir Robert Graham was determined to slay King James and Lady Catherine's arm was broken.'

'Oh . . . please . . . ' whispered Innes. 'I do not wish to hear more.'

'Why not?' asked Anna. 'It is the truth of what happened. Graham found the trap door and it was he who leaped into the vault after his men, brethren named Hall, had tried to stab their King. James cried for mercy, and Graham was shouting that he should have none since he had shown no mercy to his own kin. He shouted that the King had been hard and cruel to his barons if they dared to disobey him, and that he had humiliated the Lord of the Isles when he had asked pardon. The King's wounds were terrible . . . sixteen on his breast . . . but Graham's were even worse ere he died.'

Anna's eyes were glittering and Innes turned away.

'Small wonder that the Queen looked for revenge,' she whispered.

'Aye, but there's no need to fear her now, Mistress Jane,' said Anna, kindly. 'There is more need to fear Bess Duncan.'

'Bess Duncan!' cried Innes. 'Why should I fear Bess Duncan?'

She thought about the plump nurse-maid who also shared their sleeping quarters.

'There are men who favour tall girls with dark red hair,' said Anna, 'and you are well-born. Her mother was maidservant at Crichton Castle and her father was a nobleman, or so she claims. She craves her own establishment, but . . . ' Anna shrugged, 'she has seen the eyes of the men following you, and is jealous.'

'I want no man to look in my direction,' said Innes, quickly.

'So, you are promised?'

Anna's eyes were inquisitive.

'No.'

'But you are a Lady born. That much we can see.'

'I have no dowry.'

Anna paused, disappointed that she was receiving so little information.

'Bess claims that you answer more readily to your surname, Mistress Jane.

146

Sometimes you do not come when you are called and she finds this strange.'

This time Innes' heart missed a beat. Such a small thing, yet it had been noticed!

★ ★ ★

'I have not been a nursemaid before,' she said, quietly. 'I must learn what is expected of me.' She smiled at Anna, realising that she must make as few enemies as possible. Even Bess would have to be placated.

'If I am in error, I would be happy for you to set me right,' continued Innes.

'The great Livingstone has ridden in this morning . . . Sir Alexander Livingstone of Stirling, at the head of a party of horsemen, including his kinsman, James Livingstone. It is rumoured . . .' Anna's voice dropped, 'that he desires the guardianship of the King.'

'But Sir William Crichton . . .'

'Is Chancellor and Earl Douglas is Regent. Livingstone desires the King, but the Queen prefers to keep the boy, and Livingstone has had to accept this. But he's an ill man to cross. The Queen has bidden new men to her service. Maybe we shall see a little amusement soon. There have been no tourneys or games . . . or music and laughter this many a month.' Anna sighed and Innes chose to make her escape, saying she must help Lady Margaret.

The great hall seemed to be full of soldiers and henchmen, with maidservants providing food, and giggling behind their hands. Innes fought her way past, then suddenly she was face to face with a man out of her nightmares: and she grew pale as death, and could not tear her eyes from his face as she looked again at the coarse features, the bull neck, the heavy body and the small piglike eyes.

'Have ye seen a ghost, Mistress?' he was asking, 'or are ye struck dumb at my fine handsome countenance?'

She wanted to run outside to be sick, as, once again, the scene of carnage at

Dundallon was before her eyes. The last time she had seen him he was leading his soldiers in ravaging and killing all the women in her household, while she watched from her peephole. Any moment she expected him to recognise her; then she remembered that, whereas she had seen this man, and his fleshy face had been etched forever into her memory, he had never, in fact, seen her.

Now she tried not to shudder with revulsion.

'I am late, sir,' she said, her voice breathless with anxiety. 'I have my duties to the Queen.'

'Then I shall see you again, Mistress,' he said, his eyes roaming over her.

She pushed past and fled along the corridors to the Queen's apartments. Who was this man? It should not surprise her that the murderer of all her people should be here, in Edinburgh Castle, since he carried out his dreadful deeds in the Queen's service, but it terrified her that she might have to meet him again.

★ ★ ★

Innes became used to seeing great and powerful people arriving and departing from the castle; also to seeing the young King James II, as a boy at play, even while he was guarded as a young monarch. The red mark on his face was like a mark of distinction rather than disfigurement, and Innes could see that, although the Queen loved and cherished her daughters, her whole life was now centred on her son.

Sir Alexander Livingstone had offered to be Guardian of the young King, and had argued loudly that Sir William Crichton was already fully occupied in his position as Chancellor. Innes had no need to listen to gossip since their voices were often raised in argument. The Queen grew alarmed and called more men to her service; and it was as Innes crossed the courtyard on an errand, that her heart lurched in her breast as she saw a tall figure striding ahead of her.

'Ruari!' she cried, and he turned and stared at her, almost coldly, but not before she had seen the light leaping in his eyes.

'So you go about your duties, Mistress Innes,' he called, then drew her over to a quiet corner. 'So it is true — you wished to come to Edinburgh as a nursemaid. Is it more pleasant, then, than mistress of Glenallyn? You still have no regrets that you refused my cousin?'

She looked up at him, her heart beating wildly. 'None, sir,' she said, firmly. 'I did not love Sir Alexander.'

'Had your brother arranged it, you would have been forced.'

'Happily I felt I could choose for myself.'

She had heard a light tone in his voice and joy and laughter crinkling his eyes as he looked at her.

'I wondered if I might see you here, Mistress . . . and to think I worried about you! . . . when I knew whither you had gone. My cousin was right, and the best place to put you safely was in the Queen's service.'

This time she shook her head, but already there were other people milling around.

'How is my kinsman, Sir Alexander?' she asked, more loudly.

Ruari frowned. 'You spoiled his temper. He is warring with his neighbours, the McKinnons, over a small piece of ground no bigger than a turf. When the King was alive they would not have dared. He was aye sore on the barons quarrelling amongst themselves, and now Alexander swears he will call his men out to fight, and McKinnon says he will give him such a dunt that he will be sorry.'

'Will . . . will you be called up to aid him?' Innes asked.

'I have to serve the Queen's household for a month,' said Ruari, 'but if Earl Douglas is wise, he should be stopping these quarrels. There are too many of them breaking out, and the country becomes restless.'

'How are things at Invernairn?' asked Innes, her eyes alight. Now that she had recovered from her surprise, her heart was glowing. So Ruari was to be here for a month. She felt, too, that he was not so indifferent to her as he pretended, and his eyes had been warm as they regarded her. Now they grew a little more bleak.

'It is still a poor place, but I am working hard to set it to rights.'

'I wonder what Dundallon looks like,' she said, sadly.

'It has not been harmed,' he said, gently. 'It is a fair place and is now part of the royal estate.'

'I should hate the Queen,' she whispered in a very low voice, 'but I cannot. She has suffered much. But . . . Ruari . . . I have seen . . . '

She broke off, her eyes caught by a movement nearby and she saw that Bess Duncan was standing there, listening to every word. How much had she heard? wondered Innes with sinking heart.

'What have you seen, Mistress Innes?' Ruari was asking.

'I must go now,' said Innes, hurriedly. 'I have been away from my duties too long.'

'We will talk again,' said Ruari. 'You must know that all has not been well . . . '

But Innes only smiled and hurried to deliver her errand and return to her duties. She had always walked along the corridors, looking right and left, in case the man she hated most in the world was lurking nearby. She had learned that he was James Livingstone, a kinsman to Sir Alexander, and part of his escort. Soon Sir Alexander would be returning to Stirling and no doubt James would go with him. Innes looked forward to the day when the castle no longer housed her enemy, but now she might have cause to fear another one . . . Bess Duncan.

As Innes' feet sped along the corridor she heard Bess clattering behind her.

'Mistress Jane . . . or Mistress Innes,'

she called, 'I would have a word with you.'

Innes wished she could pretend not to have heard, but she thought it wiser to pause.

'So you have a friend among the soldiers?' Bess asked, archly.

'He is my kinsman. He is cousin to Sir Alexander Stewart who brought me here.'

'Aye, just so. A kinsman, you say? You know, Mistress Jane, I have been here some years, and I know most of the barons who have been called to serve the King . . . and the Queen. And I thought I had seen that dark red hair of yours before. It is an unusual colour and it is quite strange that others have not noticed it . . . the Queen herself even. And I remember someone else whose hair was not quite so pretty after he was punished for treason.'

Innes was white and shaking. She did not trouble to deny anything. Of what use would it have been?

'What do you want?' she asked.

Bess Duncan's lip curled a fraction, then her attitude changed.

'You can keep Master Stewart. He has nothing and it will take years for him to pull Invernairn out of the mire. If he married and fathered children, they would be in poverty all their lives. But James Livingstone has been casting eyes at you. He is different. The Livingstones are powerful, almost as powerful as the Douglases, without being so stiff-necked about their position. They think themselves the equal of royalty, do the Douglas's. James Livingstone was beginning to notice me. ME! He wants a real woman of flesh and blood and not a bit o' willow wand like you. Then you cast your golden een on him and something in the light o' them stirred his heart, and he is fluttering like the moth to the candle. Do not encourage him, Mistress Innes, that is all.'

'I can promise you that,' said Innes, eagerly. 'I would not have him if he were the last man on earth.'

But she had said the wrong thing. Bess bridled and her eyes grew cold. 'You have a fine opinion of yourself,' she said, staring Innes up and down. 'So you are not easy to please. Perhaps you will wait a wheen o' years for the King to grow up? Would that please Your Majesty?'

'I do not want anyone,' said Innes, desperately.

'Because you are so happy in the Queen's service,' said Bess with sarcasm. 'Just heed what I say, Mistress. James Livingstone will have me if he is not diverted. See that you do not tread on my toes or your pretty looks will not be enhanced.'

Innes drew a deep breath, then she turned and hurried along the corridor to help Anna.

★ ★ ★

But even Bess could not spoil her inward delight that Ruari was not so very far away. Although she only caught a brief glimpse of him now and again, since his duties were as manifold as her own, Innes took comfort from his presence.

She could have wished that James Livingstone had been kept equally busy, because the very thought of his presence made her feel physically sick. She thought about Bess Duncan's fears that she might encourage Livingstone, and the idea became more and more ludicrous. But the strain of avoiding him, when Lady Margaret sent her on an errand to the great hall, was very great, and her head seemed to jerk in all directions in order to seek his whereabouts so that she knew where he was heading and where to avoid.

He would even speak to her when she was engaged in taking the children abroad for a breath of fresh air, and her anger very often overcame her fears.

'I am on duty, sir,' she would say, with asperity, when he would have accosted her. 'I am not allowed to talk to the soldiers.'

'Come later, when you are free,' he urged. 'We can find a quiet corner in the courtyard. There is much we can . . . talk about.'

'Please go, sir,' she said, flags of colour in her cheeks.

His eyes narrowed. 'Have I known you before, Mistress?' he asked, puzzled. 'It seems to me that you are no stranger to me, and there was recognition in your eyes when they met mine.'

Innes forced herself to speak lightly. ''Tis the ordinary nature of my looks, sir,' she said, and forced a smile. 'Now if I were as distinctive as . . . as the Queen . . . you would know that we are strangers to one another.'

'You are no stranger to me,' he whispered, almost ardently. 'I admire you greatly, Mistress.'

'There is not time, sir,' she said, her very loathing lending urgency to her voice. She turned round feeling that she was being stared at, and saw that Ruari was regarding her and James Livingstone unwaveringly. Nimbly she stepped aside where he had been blocking her path, and ushered two of the younger princesses along the corridor to the Queen's apartments. If only the Castle did not require to be guarded so heavily! Even the ball game she had played with the princesses had been spoiled by the constant watch which was being kept on them.

⋆ ⋆ ⋆

Innes began to pray that James Livingstone would be recalled to Stirling, but Sir Alexander was still in Edinburgh, and the proffered friendship between the Chancellor, Sir William Crichton and himself was again wearing thin as they quarrelled about the government of the country, and in particular, the guardianship of the King.

'Sir Alexander has invited us to go to Stirling,' the Queen confided to Lady

Margaret Gordon, whilst the older Lady patiently instructed two of the princesses in needlework. 'It would be a change for us, would it not? And Stirling is a fine fortress, much like Edinburgh, being built on a rock. We would be safe there. The King would be as safe there as he is here.'

The Queen plucked nervously at her gown, though Innes could see that she was beginning to recover from the shock of her husband's death, and was now thinking more and more for her son. He was a boy to be proud of, thought Innes. He was going to be a fine soldier one day, and even now he marched up and down and shouted commands to those who would help him play his favourite game of commanding soldiers in battle.

He was also a keen huntsman and was occasionally allowed to ride to the hunt accompanied by a host of armed soldiers, but although the Queen recognised that he had to grow up fine and manly, she was nervous until he was back in the royal apartments.

Sir William accompanied the men, unwilling to allow the young King out of his sight, and sometimes Ruari would be there too, so that Innes felt that the King's safety was assured. She had almost forgotten Ruari's terrible appearance when she had first seen him, with the frightening beggar's mask on his face, and sometimes she grew afraid for him as well as herself. If the Queen were told about Ruari's other life, would she be angry with him? She had mellowed, but sometimes her lips would become thin and her eyes cold, and Innes knew that there was an indestructible streak in her which could cause her heart to harden, even where her most loyal subject was concerned.

Although the Queen had no heart for revelry, sometimes the soldiers and servants of the household would break out into merry-making and dancing, and on these occasions Innes would remain quietly in the royal apartments, knowing that it was unsafe for her to be abroad. Bess Duncan sometimes slipped away on the pretext of an errand, and came back with the smell of wine on her breath and laughter on her lips.

On one occasion she came to find Innes and beckoned her conspiratorially.

'Will ye come out into the courtyard?' she asked in a whisper, 'near to the Chapel?'

'The Chapel?' Innes asked, bewildered.

'St. Margaret's Chapel, you silly sheep,' said Bess, tittering merrily. 'He wants a word with you.'

'Who?' asked Innes.

'Your man. Do not pretend you have not got one. I told you you could keep Ruari Stewart, did I not? He is waiting for you, because he is leaving the King's service for the present, and going home. Such a home it is, too.' Bess's voice dropped again. 'They say he turned it into a shelter for beggars, and was not above begging alms himself!

Can you believe it?'

Innes swallowed and looked doubtfully at Bess, saying, 'There is revelry going on in the courtyard. I can hear the music, and the wine is flowing. Why does Master Stewart wish to see me at the Chapel when he must know it is not safe.'

'I found my way past the revellers,' said Bess with great dignity. 'Are you such a poor thing that you cannot do the same? As to meeting you by the Chapel . . . who knows but he might want the priest to perform a marriage ceremony!' Her voice dropped again. 'Is it true that you refused his cousin? Oh, but you have little sense in that head of yours, even if you exceed the princesses for beauty. Oh aye, we all admit to your being a beauty, but you are also stupid to come here and not set yourself up at Glenallyn. Now Sir Alexander — your fine kinsman — intends to wed with the Hamiltons. He needs to make a band with the Hamiltons now that he is warring with the McKinnons, so that he has friends to help him; and what better way than to marry Mary Hamilton? I expect Master Stewart will be invited to the wedding; and she will soon start breeding, and bear the good Sir Alexander an heir.'

'I do not know where you hear your gossip,' cried Innes, though secretly she enjoyed hearing about Sir Alexander. So he was going to be wed after all! Perhaps his new wife would keep him at home, and stop his skirmishes with the neighbours, instead of inducing her kin to help him! Innes did not want Ruari to be involved in these internal battles, when sometimes the barons were known to kill each other, as well as a number of fine men.

Once or twice she had managed a word with Ruari when they met within the precincts of the castle, and each time she felt that he was becoming less aloof towards her. He was working diligently so that he would be rewarded well, and his efforts would go towards restoring Invernairn. On the last occasion she had felt confident enough of his good opinion to ask about Lizzie, and this time his eyes had grown cool and he looked at her for a long moment.

'I do not discuss my servants,' he said, deliberately. 'They no longer concern you, Mistress Innes.'

A moment later he strode away, and Innes felt dejected once more. His temper was so uncertain, she thought angrily. She should no longer concern herself about him either! She was as good as he, and as well born, but he treated her like the servant she had become!

Innes had wept tears of rage and frustration that night, and had thought about her brother and her parents. How angry they would be if they could see her now. How their pride would be hurt. The thought of it had brought new backbone to her, so that she was able to pursue her duties with more authority, and the Royal children had not been allowed to do exactly as they wished. Gradually she was working out a firm but kindly discipline for them, and she felt the Queen's eyes often held approval as they rested on her.

Yet always she walked a tight-rope, with Bess Duncan hovering in the background, and now Bess wanted her to go down amongst the rabble — for such it would be — and seek out Ruari. She could not imagine that he would be taking part in too much revelry, but he would enjoy some of the fun. Amidst the hard streak which was driving him on to restore Invernairn was that other Ruari who had enjoyed being a beggar lord, and making his household follow his lead.

Innes paused only for a moment, then she went to find her cloak. The air was cold in the evenings, and the winds which blew in from the North Sea chilled one to the bone. She met Anna Gourlay as she came out of her apartment.

'Where are you going, Jane?' the older girl asked, alarm in her voice. 'You must know that it is not fit for you to go amongst that rabble.'

'I . . . Master Stewart wishes to talk with me,' said Innes. 'Bess Duncan has brought a message.'

'Bess Duncan!' cried Anna. 'You must have taken leave o' your wits, Jane Innes. She would not bring you such a message unless there was mischief behind it.'

'He is returning to Invernairn,' said Innes, 'and wishes to take his leave of me. You know we are not permitted to talk with the soldiers, and it would be noticed if I tried to see him in the morning.'

'He means much to you?' Anna asked.

'I have few friends other than Master Stewart . . . and yourself,' said Innes, and Anna's expression softened.

'Go, then, but go carefully, and I will cover for you if you are needed. But do not stay out long in the snell winds even if your heart is warm. Lady Margaret might wish to see if you are a-bed. Bess Duncan was beaten for going amongst the revellers last time, though she risks much for the feel of a man's arms round her. Where is she now?'

'She is waiting for me,' said Innes. 'I must go to the Lady's Chapel which is quiet, since none dare disturb the peace there.'

'I do not like it,' Anna frowned, 'but go if you must.'

'I will be careful,' said Innes.

She stole quietly along the corridor, her heart in her mouth, in case Lady Margaret should see her. It would mean a beating if she were discovered, and her limbs were more delicate than Bess's firm buttocks.

'You have taken long enough,' Bess snarled as they sped down the stone stairs together. 'Master Stewart will think twice about waiting for one so tardy, and will choose another more willing.' She sniggered. 'I would not be unwilling, myself, for a man of his charms, though he glowers too often for my liking. They say he once broke a man's arm for ill-treating his horse.

Come, Mistress Innes . . . through this doorway and we will avoid the roisterers. They have been kept down too long, and have sickened of seeing men tried and condemned, and of hearing their cries from the prisons. They make merry in order to shut out the sounds from their ears. The Queen understands this, and whereas she does not condone, she does not condemn either, but stays silent. Only we who are close to her are punished; but I can take my punishment if I have had my fill of pleasure. Come, Mistress Innes, some ale will help you to part with your lover. It will warm and soften you, since you are no more than a piece of glass.'

Innes shook her head. 'The ale is cheap,' she said. 'It would sicken me. Where do we go now, Bess.'

'Over here,' said a rough voice, and a moment later Innes was being held as though in a vice, while Bess burst into hysterical laughter.

'You have done well, Bess Duncan,' the man was saying. 'I shall not forget you, never fear; but now I must deal with the apple which escaped the barrel. From somewhere she saw me. I know it now. It was in her eyes.'

The night was dark, but torches had been lit and there were groups of people dancing, singing, laughing and slopping ale around. Innes thought that it looked like a scene out of Hell as she was crushed against the bull-like strength of James Livingstone.

'Be off with you,' he growled to Bess. 'I will take my time over these pleasures.'

His hand had been over Innes' mouth, but now that he had removed it she moaned a little then tried to scream. A moment later his thick lips had claimed hers, whilst his hand held the back of her neck. Innes felt that she could have died with revulsion as she felt his male hardness pressing against her body. There was the nauseating smell of cheap ale on his breath, and his other hand was tearing at her clothing as he pressed her up against a wall.

'So you thought to escape, my bird, did you?' he snarled. One of the torches had been stuck into a holder on the wall, and in its pale flickering light his face looked like the Devil himself. Innes felt that the nightmare, stemming from the first time she had seen James Livingstone, was being multiplied many times. This could not be happening to her, she thought, her body numb with shock; then fear lent her strength as his hands reached their goal, and she began to struggle like a wildcat.

'No sense in struggling, little kitten,' said Livingstone silkily. 'I could throw you to the ground and have you like I had the Lady of Dundallon, but I am determined that you will enjoy me; then — who knows? — I may spare you to be my playmate until you cease to please me. Soon we return to Stirling, with the Royal Family . . . on a visit!' He laughed as he pulled her towards him again, and Innes could hear only evil in the sound. 'There are quiet corners in Edinburgh, but we would have more comfort at Stirling, Mistress Frazer.'

Innes, exhausted, had paused in her struggles but James Livingstone's next move caused her to thrust him back with renewed vigour. She succeeded in hurting him and he swore viciously. She reached out blindly and her fingers encountered the torch, and a moment later she had jabbed it into his cheek.

He howled with pain and she crashed it down on his head, so that he slumped to the ground.

All was in darkness, but Innes could hear Bess Duncan beginning to scream. Her own senses seemed to be leaving her and she was violently sick; then people were running from all directions, and from the shadows Anna Gourlay ran over to grab her arm and drag her well away from the scene.

'I knew it was a trap, Mistress Jane,' she was saying urgently. 'She brought you to a soldier to be brutalised.'

'He . . .'

Innes knew there was something she

should tell Anna, but she did not know what it was. She could hear Bess Duncan screeching, and her name called through mists of pain and sickness. Then after an eternity, Anna was back with her again amidst the confusion.

'Over here,' Anna was saying to someone. 'Lift her gently, but you had better take her to Master Stewart. He will know what to do. She is his kinswoman and if the man really is Master James Livingstone there will be trouble. Take this gown and cloak — hide her. Here they come, so go now.'

Innes was aware of one or two men muttering in low voices, and the smell of ale seemed to be all around her again. Others were shouting for more torches to be brought, but a moment later she was thrown up on to a horse, and the smell of leather and horseflesh was in her nostrils; then she knew no more.

7

When Innes woke the moon was up and the night air was like a douche of cold water in her face. There was a smell of woodsmoke nearby, and she found that she was lying huddled in Anna's cloak and one or two evil-smelling blankets.

Nearby, four men were talking in low voices, and she recognised that they were henchmen, but had no idea to whom they owed allegiance.

She moaned a little with the pain of her stomach after her sickness, and a moment later one of their number came to look down on her, and she saw a rough bearded face with greying hair, and kindly eyes.

'Who . . . who are you?' she whispered. 'What happened? Oh . . . '

Remembrance was with her again, and she shuddered with fear at the thought that she had felled James Livingstone. Her hands were burned with the torch, and the pain seemed to sear her body.

'I . . . I killed a man,' she whispered with horror.

'Nay, Mistress, he is not dead,' the man said, almost jovially. 'Master Livingstone's head is made of harder stuff, but you will have spoiled his beauty for many a long day, if not for ever. I examined him and he has a scorch mark on his cheeks which will not heal in a hurry. But he is a powerful man in the land, Mistress, and will want his revenge.'

Innes shuddered, and accepted gratefully when the man offered her a hot drink of some sort of herbal mixture.

'Who are you and why have you brought me here? Where are we?' she asked.

The other three men were now standing nearby, and once again Innes felt fear clawing at her.

'There is no need to fear us,

Mistress,' the first man said, gently. 'Ye canna see us properly since it is too dark, but ye have seen us before. We were beggars together under Master Stewart. We are from Invernairn, and have been ordered by the master to return there. He rode to Glenallyn with the rest of the men yesterday, but we were allowed to stay for the revels.'

Innes was almost weak with relief, so that the tears were suddenly flowing and she drew great shuddering sobs.

'Hush, Mistress Frazer,' the man was saying. 'You will need all your courage, Lady, because Master Livingstone will be like a demented bull to find you, and by now it will be known you are Sir Archibald Frazer's sister. You will not be in full favour at the court.'

'Where are we?' she asked, taking hold of herself.

'We are using a little-known route back to Invernairn. We cross the mountains, and the air will be cold but there is little fear of pursuit. I am Will Munro, ma'am . . . '

'Lizzie's Uncle Will?'

'The same. Thomas, here, has found a rabbit and is cooking a fine stew. It will warm us and give us strength, but ye maun eat out o' the same pot as us men. There are no niceties when we have to leave in a hurry. Fortunately the guard was enjoying the revelry and we had a pass to leave the garrison. We were not stopped, but when James Livingstone sobers up his men, they will soon add up what has happened. But we would have to answer to Master Ruari if we did not care for you, Mistress. He says you are kin to him.'

Innes nodded. It was easier to claim such a kinship than to explain further.

'But . . . how did you know I was in trouble,' she asked.

'I know Mistress Anna Gourlay, and she recognised the men from Invernairn. She was quick to help you.'

'She will be punished,' said Innes, painfully. 'Maybe I should go back.'

'You canna help her,' said Will Munro, 'and her punishment will be light compared with your own. Eat up, Mistress, you need strength to your bones.'

'Do you take me to Invernairn or to Glenallyn? asked Innes.

There was silence for a while. 'They will search both from end to end,' said Will Munro, 'if they get the chance. Glenallyn is well defended, but Invernairn . . . Invernairn will have to be defended against Livingstone.'

'Oh.' Innes lost some of her appetite as she began to see the repercussions of all that had happened.

'You must not be found in either. We can truthfully say that you are not within the walls, if we take you somewhere else. Have you no friends who would hide you, Mistress?'

Innes shook her head slowly.

'My uncles were killed in battle before they could marry . . . and my father . . . and my brother lost all his family. He should never have raised his hand against the King,' she said. 'The country has become lawless since his death.'

'Aye, now Livingstone and Crichton are like dogs over a bone.'

Will refilled his plate with stew. 'The Livingstones mean to have the King, because they think that whoever guards his Majesty wields the power. And Crichton is determined to look after the Queen, since he was such a great friend to James the First, but without the support of that strong King behind him, he is weak. As is the powerful Douglas. He is a great baron, but a weak man. Everywhere the barons are quarrelling and sniping at one another, and Sir Alexander Frazer is as bad as any. That is why Master Ruari is called to Glenallyn. Sir Alexander is lying there wounded, but he will be out fighting the McKinnons again as soon as he is on the mend. When tempers start to rise, they take a lot o' cooling.'

'Will . . . will Master Stewart be fighting?' asked Innes, half-fearfully, and there was silence. She remembered again that Livingstone would look for her at Invernairn and Ruari would have to fight to keep Invernairn from the torch.

She would have to hide somewhere, thought Innes. But where?

'Did you return Janet Balfour to her daughter's home at Leyburn?' she asked. 'Meg and Thomas Bell . . . tenant farmers . . . near to where Master Stewart found us when he went a-begging?'

'That we did, Mistress,' said Will, heartily. 'We were aye particular who we begged from, and no one was molested. Even if we made a lot o' noise, we only begged for food and clothing to keep Invernairn alive, and a few merks that rich folk could well spare. We returned Mistress Balfour to her daughter's farmstead with food for their stomachs.'

'I will go there,' said Innes.

'It is not a place for a lady like you,' said Will, doubtfully.

'It is a place for anyone if it affords shelter and . . . sanctuary. All other places of sanctuary will be searched.'

Will nodded. 'We will take you there,

Mistress. If the Queen goes to Stirling they will have other things to think about than finding you; though James Livingstone will aye be your enemy.'

'He was my enemy from the first time I saw him,' said Innes.

But she knew he was now Ruari Stewart's enemy as well.

They moved slowly over the mountains while the air grew colder and the chill mists swept on top of them. Innes' gown had been torn by James Livingstone, but she had a plain garment which Anna had thrust under her cloak, and she adjusted her clothing to cover herself as warmly as she could. The cloak gave great warmth and comfort, and Will Munro found her a thick blanket for nights, though the bracken shelters which the men built afforded fine protection against the elements.

For Innes it was a time to recover all her senses, and to shake off the numb feeling which followed the shock of all that had happened to her. But with the return of strength, her nerves again grew jangled and her hands began to shake, so that she was startled by the slightest noise. The mountain path was lonely, but occasionally they disturbed a wild creature which bounded in front of the horses causing them to rear, whilst Innes' heart fluttered with fright.

Occasionally, too, they would see a party of horsemen in the distance, and knew that one of the barons was probably travelling abroad, or perhaps soldiers were travelling on the King's business. Will always bade the party halt whilst he scanned the horizon for any signs of pursuit, but as each day passed and they made slow careful progress, he was more and more convinced that this winding detour would be the shortest route to Invernairn in the final analysis.

Then one morning Innes woke to find a clear blue sky and the faint warmth of pale sunshine on her face, lighting up the bushes of birch and hazel, and the great grey boulders and sweet heather which grew mistily out of the mountains. Above her a curlew called plaintively, and a long-legged heron flapped its way towards a clear brown trout stream. The faint murmur of the stream was sad and rather mournful, but for once Innes' heart was no longer so heavy as she smelled a pot of meat cooking over a fire which one of the men had lit.

Normally Innes had small appetite, but this morning she was hungry and longed for some of the dainty food which had been served in the Royal household.

The Queen and her ladies had gradually been recovering their appetites, and the cooks had had to put aside their slovenly habits and serve up food fit for the Queen and her children to eat. The King's food was all prepared separately, and well tested before being offered to him. He was often heard to complain that it had grown cold, but it was small price to pay for ensuring that it was also nourishing.

'How far have we to go now, Will?' Innes asked. 'I am unused to the saddle and have been weary, but now I can sense a change in the air. I fancied I could smell peat burning.'

'We should see Invernairn before the sun is at its height,' Will promised, 'and it is no distance to deliver you to Meg Bell's farmstead. You will be able to rest and shelter round a fire this very night, never fear, Mistress, though I doubt that a soft bed will await you at Leyburn.'

'I am content to wait,' said Innes, happily, 'and any bed would be soft after the saddle. Oh Will, I do not think that the soldiers will come for me now. We must have shaken them off. And do you not think that James Livingstone will now be required to go to Stirling with Sir Alexander, in order to ensure the Queen's comfort and proper quarters for the King. Surely he will have too much to do to trouble about me. Perhaps the sore head I gave him will be better now.'

A sense of well being was dispelling her nightmares.

'Aye, and mebby heuch-aye,' said Will, at which Innes looked puzzled and had to ask him to explain. Will's speech was not always easy to follow.

'Maybe aye and maybe no,' he repeated. 'It would tak' a great prophet to see what is in the mind of yon man.'

Innes grew more subdued and silent. The fresh air and exercise had given her such a fine sense of security but it was only wishful thinking. She was still in deep trouble.

As they rode nearer to Invernairn, Will Munro grew ever more cautious, reining in to scan the horizon, and investigating rocky boulders which could provide a hiding place for an ambush. He avoided woodland paths and skirted the woods keeping close to the trees; then as they were within easy reach of Invernairn, he brought the party to a halt, his keen nose sniffing the air.

'Something is alight,' he said and a moment later Innes, too, could smell the acrid scent of burning vegetation.

'Livingstone . . . that cateran!'

Will spurred his horse and they proceeded at a gallop, forgetful of all precautions as they rounded a corner and saw, in the distance, the smouldering ruins of Invernairn.

'The caterans have burned us out,' cried Will, his eyes bulging with anger, 'for a second time! First the auld master and now his son. Oh, I tell you, someone will pay dearly for this work.'

The other men's voices rumbled with oaths, and they forgot about Innes and spurred their horses into making the shortest possible time to Invernairn.

Her eyes were wide with horror as she began to realise the implications. Where was Ruari, and what had happened to him? Was he now being punished, after all his efforts to rebuild Invernairn, for the injury she had inflicted on James Livingstone? And what about Glenallyn? Was Sir Alexander Frazer, too, paying a terrible price for claiming that she was kin?

As they rode into Invernairn the air

grew heavy with smoke, and the men dismounted hastily, then began to search amidst the ruins. Tired-looking men, with blood on their clothing had rescued what they could of Ruari Stewart's dearly-bought new possessions after putting out the fire. In the great hall, wounded men and women were lying on make-shift beds of reeds and blankets, whilst out in the courtyard a more gruesome sight met Innes' horrified gaze.

She ran back to the great hall and saw one woman in ragged clothing, bending over a henchman to wet his parched lips, and she recognised Lizzie.

'Lizzie!' cried Innes. 'Oh Lizzie! What . . . what happened? Was Livingstone here . . . or just his men?' Can you tell me what happened?'

Lizzie turned to stare at her like a wildcat. 'You happened!' she cried. 'Here she is, the Jezebel. It was you they wanted, Mistress Frazer, and they burned Invernairn round our ears to find you, and murdered our men and women and children to find you . . . '

'Let be, Lizzie,' croaked old Hannah, shuffling up to her with a bowl of warm water. 'She wasna here. It wasna the fault o' the young Mistress.'

'Where is Master Stewart?' asked Innes.

'It is the Maister's turn next,' Lizzie told her, eyes glittering. 'He is at Glenallyn. They have ridden off in a rage to destroy Glenallyn as well as Invernairn.'

'Oh no!' cried Innes. 'Oh . . . Will . . . where is Will? We must go to Glenallyn, Will, and . . . warn Master Stewart.'

'How stupid you are, Mistress Frazer,' said Lizzie, her lip curling. 'How do you think to be in Glenallyn before Livingstone's men?'

'It is too late, Mistress,' said Will, heavily, 'and if you wish to aid Master Stewart, it would be better if we took you to Meg Bell's farmstead and left you there. No one will look for you in that place. Livingstone's men have flayed about them in a rage when they did not find you, but it would have been as nothing if they had found you, and punished Invernairn for giving you sanctuary. They do not know you are under our protection, and might think you are a-wandering and hiding on your own; even hiding around the township of Edinburgh. There would be rumours after our party rode out, but only Mistress Anna knows for certain. They might be thinking twice when they did not find you here, and Glenallyn is well guarded, so do not trouble yourself further, Mistress.'

'She brings ruin wherever she goes,' said Lizzie, bitterly.

'Cannot I help you to bandage the wounded?' asked Innes. She did not mind Lizzie's rantings. They were as nothing compared with the wrath of Livingstone.

'We must not forget what a fine Lady you are,' said Lizzie. 'Will ye also help us to beg for our meat again?'

'I will,' said Innes, steadily and Lizzie

was silenced. Then Lizzie began to walk away with the painful gait of one who has been cruelly assaulted; one who would have shared Lady Eleanor's fate but for her superb strength.

'Oh, Lizzie, I am sorry!' cried Innes, and again the other girl turned to look at her, but now there was only understanding between them.

'Go with my Uncle Will,' Lizzie ordered. 'You can do nothing here but set us in danger by your presence. They may come back if they've had wind o' ye. Get away from here, Mistress.'

Innes nodded. There was nothing she could do. She looked at the blackened ruins, and remembered how proud Ruari Stewart had been that it was all being built up again. She remembered his service to the Royal household and how diligently he had worked; even though it must have irked him to be away from Invernairn, and not able to watch the old keep being rebuilt day by day. Now it was all gone again, and when he knew the whole story he was going to hate her.

She walked towards the small room Ruari had given her, wondering if there were any garments still left there which she could wear; but it was empty and blackened.

Slowly she returned to Will Munro, who was giving comfort to old Hannah.

'I will leave with you whenever you wish, Will,' she said. 'I cannot stay here. Lizzie is right. I am just an added threat to all of you.'

'First we will make a meal,' said Will, 'and feed the wounded with broth. We need victuals ourselves, Mistress Innes, and the horses must be rested.'

'I . . . I could not eat,' she whispered. 'I have no appetite.'

'You can eat a bit o' broth,' said Hannah, sharply. 'Will is right. Some may die of their wounds, but it makes no sense to die o' hunger. Come on. Lizzie, we hae work to do.'

8

Innes felt strange and heartsick as they rode on to Dundallon land once again. Gradually she had realised that if Will and his men had taken the shortest route to Invernairn, they would have helped to protect it from Livingstone. They had protected her, but at what a cost!

Now it seemed an eternity since she used to ride about Dundallon with Archibald or Eleanor, to visit friends and oversee the estate. There had been many farms, tenanted by good farmers who owed allegiance to Archibald, but now she could see signs of neglect in the uncultivated soil and the few animals who roamed the fields. Without a baron at the castle, the tenant farmers were lazy about digging their plots, even though they still owed rent for their farms, and it would be required to be paid to the Crown.

Sometimes it had been paid with sheep or grain, Innes remembered, but Archibald had been lenient over payment; though he liked to run his estate within the law of the land, giving fair judgement when he had to hold court, and seeing to it that the farms were well-run and provided good food and shelter for the people. In return the tenant farmers were asked to support Archibald in the event of a quarrel with a neighbour; but Archibald had spent his time mainly away from the estate in visiting Graham and his friends. He had not made quarrels with his neighbours.

He had organised wolf hunts, however, and had paid twopence for every whelp's head. He had commanded his farmers to kill the crows which damaged their crops, and had seen to it that every man from sixteen to sixty could use a weapon according to his rank; and Innes had often begged to be allowed to join the boys who fired at a target placed near the church when they foregathered every holiday. Lady Eleanor had been very displeased with her, and she had been beaten soundly when it was discovered that she had joined the throng of young men and admiring females to watch each one shooting his three arrows at a target.

One of the soldiers had shouted encouragement, then roared his disappointment when the arrows missed their mark.

'Ye canna shoot even if I were to offer a honeycake to have you hit the target.'

'Gie me a good sword any day,' the boy had cried, boldly, 'or a battle-axe.'

'The English will shoot ye down before ye can get it into yer hand,' he was told. 'Ye can all use a sword, but you must learn to shoot your arrows.'

The echoes of those days seemed to ring in Innes' ears as she rode past the places she had loved so much, and her heart ached because of the forlorn appearance and the neglect she saw there. Soon, perhaps, the Queen would take up her business affairs, or pass them on to Sir William Crichton, and Dundallon would be cared for once more. Meanwhile . . . meanwhile the last of the Frazers was going to hide out in one of the meanest of the farmsteads.

They noticed three children playing around the door, which was, they were glad to see, a wooden structure and not an ox-hide as was used on some of the poorer cottages.

'It looks a poor place,' said Will, reining in. 'Maybe . . . maybe there is somewhere else ye could go, Mistress. Surely some fine lady would give ye shelter?'

'There is nobody,' said Innes, shaking her head.

Who amongst them would have supported Archibald when he helped to murder the King? Who would be friend to her now?

Will looked on her forlorn face and frowned. All his life he had been a retainer at Invernairn, and had mixed with others of his kind who stood together in trouble as they were taught in church. The nobility had deaf ears to the church's teaching, he thought, since they dealt so harshly with a young maid. They should not be turning their faces away from her.

Yet how would Thomas Bell receive one of her kind without recompense? He was not a good farmer and could scarcely keep his brood already. He would hardly welcome a lady of her quality.

Will frowned, then put the thoughts behind him. He had more to worry him at the moment. They had told him at Invernairn that Livingstone's men had gone to Glenallyn, but he comforted himself with the thought that Glenallyn was well guarded and in good trim, since Sir Alexander decided to teach his neighbours a lesson. They would not find it so easy as Invernairn, but he was still going to have to explain himself to Master Ruari . . .

He urged his party forward towards the farmstead known as Leyburn.

'There is much to do, so we had best

leave you in good hands, Mistress,' he said.

The children stood watching them, then ran indoors to inform their mother. A moment later Meg Bell stood in the doorway, her eyes widening with fear when she saw the horsemen.

Will dismounted and helped Innes from the saddle then he led her forward.

'Will ye give sanctuary to Mistress Frazer of Dundallon?'

Meg stared at Innes, the colour draining from her cheeks.

'Dundallon is a garrison and is being held for the Crown,' she said. 'We are just poor folk and have no room for sanctuary.'

Innes stepped forward. 'You know me, Meg,' she said. 'Where is your mother, Janet Balfour? Is she well?'

'She is . . . ' Meg hesitated, 'by the fireside. My mother is an old woman who can help nobody.'

There was a heavy footstep and Thomas Bell lumbered round the corner. They all stared at him as he slowly moved forward, his face dull and lowering.

'There is no room for Mistress Frazer,' he said. 'We owe allegiance to the Crown, and not to any Frazer. They are outlawed, if any are left, and are put to the horn.'

'I am all that is left,' said Innes, clearly. 'If you do not welcome me, I shall go.'

'And Thomas Bell is a fool,' said Will Munro.

'A fool, is it?' the man asked. 'I would be a great fool if I burdened myself with an outlawed woman who is liable to bring the soldiers on us at any time.'

'She is outlawed now,' said Will, 'but royal hearts can change as quick as lightning. Master Stewart of Invernairn was outlawed because his father was put to the horn, but now he is in favour. If Mistress Frazer is returned to favour, she may think you do not deserve the tenancy of Leyburn. What say you, Mistress Frazer?'

'I tell ye, I have no meat to fill her belly,' cried Thomas Bell. He had a rough, guttural tongue and Innes had difficulty in following his words, but she understood his meaning. She thought longingly of the merks which she had sewn inside her own cloak and of the rest of her clothing left in a chest at Edinburgh. No doubt Bess Duncan would have claimed them by now, but if she had done so, maybe it would put a quieter tongue in her head. She would not wish to be accused of the theft of the coins, and would not draw too much attention to herself.

Then her mind went to the strongbox full of Eleanor's jewellery that she had buried in a recess under the banks of the stream, not far from Leyburn. There was enough there in gold to keep her fed and clothed for many a day, though she had planned to give it to Ruari to atone for this new loss.

'Do not worry,' she said, wearily. 'You will be paid. I would like to see Janet Balfour.'

'She is a doddering auld woman,' said Thomas Bell. 'She wanders in her mind.'

'I would like to see her,' Innes insisted.

'The Mistress should be given sanctuary and welcome, Thomas,' said Meg, her eyes on Will. He had talked sense from her point of view. The nobles were aye at war with one another, and making bands, then breaking them, so that you never knew who to support. The Crown now owned their land, but suppose it was returned to the Frazers. Where would they be then? The Mistress was young, but if she married, her lord might oversee her affairs. And besides, there was a glint in her eyes which showed that she was no weakling. Her mother, Janet Balfour, had said that Mistress Innes was a wayward child at times. Besides, had she not just said they would be paid? Meg's eyes grew greedy for possible rewards.

'Yer're daft, woman,' Thomas Bell growled. 'A young Lady and an auld woman and a brood o' bairns. Where will a man find peace in his home?'

'There is little peace in it when you are at the fireside,' said Meg.

'Haud yer tongue or I just might cut it out for ye.'

Innes turned away. How could she stay here? She looked imploringly at Will, but his mind was firmly fixed on his duties to his master. The farmstead was a hovel, but all the safer for that. Livingstone's men were hardly likely to look for Mistress Frazer in such a place.

'Will ye tak' her?' he asked Thomas Bell, 'or do I have to ask ye again?'

This time there was steel in his voice.

'I'll tak' her,' said Thomas, as they measured one another. 'No ill feelings so long as the Lady sups from the same pot. We canna make niceties for her.'

'I am no longer used to niceties,' said Innes. 'I have supped from a communal pot before.'

'Come away then,' Meg invited, 'and see my mother. She is wandering in her mind since a wee while after this man brought her here from Dundallon.'

'I brought ye enough food for an

army,' Will reminded her.

'I have bairns to feed,' said Thomas Bell. 'It did not last for ever.'

'Take the Lady indoors, Meg Bell,' said Will, and reached out to take hold of Thomas Bell. Innes could hear the low menacing note in his voice as he talked to the farmer. Will's temper could only stand so much, then he lost patience. She knew that he could strike fear into most men, and that she would have little trouble from Thomas Bell.

Inside the farmhouse, Innes found it so dark that she could scarcely see. There was a sickly smell of dirt and unwashed human beings, and when her eyes grew accustomed to the light, she saw the outline of Janet Balfour sitting in a corner of the room.

'She keeps sitting on her box of possessions she brought with her,' said Meg. 'Your box maybe, Mistress. She thinks we are going to steal her other bits and pieces, but who would want the rubbish she treasures? She has a coloured shawl she would not be allowed to wear since it is against the law. We only wear homespun and little o' that. I think she has some o' your gowns, Mistress, but she guards them night and day, and is feared I will take them.'

Innes scarcely listened. She ran over to the old woman and dropped on her knees on the bare hardened earth floor.

'Oh Janet,' she whispered. 'Janet, I'm so glad to see you again.'

'Wha . . . wha is it?' the old woman croaked. 'Is it the Lady . . . Lady Eleanor? Never fear, ma'am, I will look to you. I will see ye right.'

'No, it's Mistress Innes, not Lady Eleanor,' said Meg.

'They took Mistress Innes,' Janet said, dully. 'I will look to Lady Eleanor.'

She stared at Innes whose eyes had filled with tears.

'You are not the Lady,' she said at length. 'You are one o' them. They beggars. They canna touch me. I will stay here.'

'She will not leave her corner, but for a walk to the midden,' said Meg, frankly, 'and I think we would be accused of trying to murder her if we were to touch her treasures. I got a look in the box and saw the clothing and the shawl she holds to her, but I wouldna touch her poor bit things, and I will not let Thomas Bell touch them either. She is my mother. Try and talk to her, Mistress, now and again, and maybe she will remember and be herself again. It will come back to her.'

'Poor Janet!' said Innes. 'I had not expected to find her like this.'

Meg threw some wood on to the fire, which blew out smoke over the room, making Innes' eyes sting, though Janet and Meg showed no signs of disturbance, being used to the smoke.

'There is no sea coal left,' she said. 'We can beg some at the church if it grows too cauld. The wood is green.'

The four children had crept in, three boys who had been playing outside when Innes arrived, and a girl of about two years who had been sleeping in a bed of hay.

'It is a bit o' hare stew for our meat,' said Meg, brushing a stray hair out of her eyes. 'Rough meat for a Lady, but all we have.'

'It is sufficient, thank you,' said Innes, rather dully.

Now that she was becoming used to the gloom, she could see the poverty and squalor of her surroundings. She had often visited the farmsteads with Lady Eleanor when a tenant farmer was in need of help, and a good housewife could make even the poorest hovel neat and cleanly swept. But Meg was a slattern, thought Innes. If she were going to stay here for very long, she would have to see that the house was cleaned.

Innes' heart was heavy. She would have to stay here. There was nowhere else for her to go.

*   *   *

It seemed to Innes that she had been at Leyburn for an eternity. Every hour was like a day; every minute an hour. She found out that the well was a distance from the farmstead, and that it was not easy for Meg to find time to carry water for cleaning.

Thomas Bell was a free tenant farmer, but the Leyburn land was poor and sour so that his crops were small, and there was little left after he had paid his portion of them in rent.

His cattle did not thrive, and he was too indolent to dig the plot of land each day as required by law. He had owed allegiance to Sir Archibald Frazer and had sometimes ridden out to fight when one of the few quarrels broke out. Since he employed no labour other than his family, he took no part in wolf hunts, and was therefore obliged to pay the fine of a sheep instead of earning himself twopence for each whelp's head.

Innes had had little idea that any farmer could live so ill, and when hunger gnawed at her healthy young body, she demanded of Meg when the cooking pot was likely to be hung over the fire.

'There is no meat, Mistress,' Meg said, sulkily. 'We do not eat meat every day.'

'Then what do you have?'

'A boil up of soup . . . if I can find ocht to put into it.'

The soup was tasteless and far from satisfying but Meg's children ate it hungrily. Their father hounded them to work on the farm with loud oaths and a threatening arm, but he soon ran out of energy so that the three small boys and their baby sister were soon playing in the mud, their clothing ragged and their faces scarcely wiped.

Innes, who had been taught her lessons even though she was a girl, innocently wondered when they did their learning from the priest; and Meg laughed shrilly and wondered which baron had fathered the brats.

As the days slowly passed and Meg grew more sullen, Innes learned more and more about the life of a tenant farmer who was too poor to become fat.

'Thomas Bell could learn a few

lessons from the other farmers,' she remarked to Meg one day. She had offered to instruct the children since the monks seemed to be so lax about teaching the poor, and received a surly answer for her pains. They would be required to learn only how to use a bow and arrow when they came of age, and how to avoid the occasional blow until then.

Innes had felt rebuffed by Thomas' surly manner, and she seethed with indignation. He would not have dared to treat her so if Dundallon had not been taken for the Crown. As it was, he had to be reminded by Meg now and again that the young Mistress was a Lady born and not a maid-servant they had hired, even though Innes had offered to do her share of chores, and felt that the farmstead was the sweeter for her efforts.

Old Janet still stared at her with vacant eyes, which sometimes grew bright with knowledge when she would call Innes 'Lady Eleanor' and cling to her arm excitedly. She left her corner rarely, but Innes had managed to bring water from the well and make her more clean and wholesome. Janet had always been clean in her habits and had attended to Innes' clothes. When she staggered off towards the privy one day, Innes had quickly looked into the chest she guarded so carefully, and found her own gowns lying on top of Janet's treasures. The old woman must have been carrying them that terrible evening when they left Dundallon.

Innes was glad to remove the tattered garment which required to be washed, and put on one of the gowns. It was of a bright primrose colour and Meg looked at it fearfully.

'Best not go outside wearing that, Mistress,' she said.

'Why not?' asked Innes. She had worn it many times whilst travelling round the estate.

'You know very fine that farmers canna wear bright colours, but only homespun. You will be seen and the soldiers will be here like a bolt o' lightning.'

Innes looked down at the pretty gown. It had given her pleasure to wear something of her own which was not torn and dirty, but Meg was right. It would only draw attention to herself.

Slowly she removed the garment and pulled on her tattered gown once more, placing the yellow one back in the chest.

'Shall I search the hedgerows for wild fruit since the fields are going back to nature for want of attention?' she asked Meg.

'Haud yer tongue, young Mistress,' said Meg, suddenly losing her temper. 'Ye decry Thomas Bell who gives you shelter, but you do not see that he is weak from lack o' nourishment, and canna dig his plot on an empty belly. He has no ox to help him plough, and he maun pay rent wi' food that could fill our bellies. And now he must feed my mother and . . . and yourself, Mistress. Twa more mouths mean less for the bairns and himself. Maybe he sounds crabbit and surly, but he has a right to be crabbit, that's all I can say.'

'Oh Meg!' Innes looked at her, horrified. Somehow she had never really considered where food came from. Always it had been there, on the table, for her to eat, and in Edinburgh it had been as dainty and plentiful as she could wish, when the Queen was being served. She had thought that if Thomas had no time to dig his plot, he could merely kill a sheep for the pot. It had not occurred to her that the sheep were as scarce as other commodities.

'Could Thomas sell a necklace of gold for me?' she asked Meg, 'or maybe exchange it for food and clothing?'

'What necklace, Mistress?' asked Meg, looking at her tattered clothing.

'I can find it,' said Innes.

'He would be accused of stealing.'

Innes bit her lip. It was true. How could Thomas Bell explain how he had come by a piece of jewellery? Innes had not examined the strongbox, but she knew that it contained valuable pieces, and might also contain gold coins, and those would be easier to exchange.

Meg was looking at her suspiciously.

'I have no merks, Meg,' she confessed. 'They were sewn into my clothing which was left in Edinburgh . . . when when the soldiers were searching for me . . . '

Meg paled. She had not been curious as to what had happened to Innes prior to her arrival, and Innes had said nothing. Meg had assumed that she had been held at Invernairn, then released when she was able to pay ransom; or had convinced the beggars that she was able to pay. She had presumed that Innes' merks had gone there.

'Hae the soldiers been sent from Edinburgh, Mistress?' she asked. 'Great heavens, they could kill us a' if they find ye here. I thocht it was just Stewart of Invernairn you had to fear.'

Innes bit her lip to stop it trembling at the mention of Ruari's name. 'I do not think I have to fear Invernairn,' she said, 'but I offended James Livingstone, Meg, kinsman to Livingstone of Stirling. He . . . he would have . . . '

'Aye, I know what he would hae done to ye, Mistress,' said Meg, then threw her head in the direction of the children.

'My eldest was forced on me by some noble who came to Dundallon in the old maister's time. It might have gone hard for me if Bell had not taken me to wife.'

'But surely my father would have helped you, or my brother?'

Meg's mouth twisted. 'A kitchen wench . . . a child o' Janet Balfour's . . . what am I but a slave to be sold if the maister thinks fit. Thomas Bell had to ask for me and offer to pay in rent.'

Innes was silent. Every day she learned new things, and she grew more appalled by her knowledge. She had boxed the ears of slatternly maids in her brother's house, when they might have been weak or ill. They might have gone in fear of guests who wished for pleasure after drinking Archibald's strong wines and ales. The retainers had been housed and fed at Dundallon, and they had worked to keep the life of the castle moving, but now they were dead, and in death they were more real to Innes as she lived out each day so close to poverty. She was only just beginning to understand what their lives had been like.

'I am sorry, Meg,' she mumbled. 'I . . . maybe I have been unfeeling to some poor maidservants.'

'It is well enough,' said Meg. 'They would not respect you had it been otherwise. They would need you as you need them. But now you have no merks, Mistress, and cannot get them from Edinburgh, because we will hae to sup from nettles and dandelions before Thomas Bell goes to Edinburgh for your merks, Mistress.'

'I had not even thought about it, Meg,' said Innes. 'My merks are gone, but I have got a strongbox of valuables which belonged to the Lady Eleanor.'

Meg's eyes sharpened. 'Where is it,

Mistress Innes?'

'Buried under the banks of a stream. Janet and I buried it, hoping that I could go back for it after we had settled down somewhere . . . here, perhaps. We buried it before the beggars found us, but I could find it again, Meg. The box contains precious ornaments for adornment and . . . and such things that were valuable to Lady Eleanor. Perhaps the jewels would not help us because we could not sell them, but there could be gold coins in the box, though I do not know for certain.'

'Gold coins!' Meg's eyes had brightened. 'Thomas could do much wi' a gold coin . . . '

'Do not be too hopeful, Meg,' Innes cautioned. 'I did not examine the contents of the box, but it could be so. Tomorrow I will take the road for Dundallon and look for the box.'

'Thomas would go with you Mistress. You could not go alone.'

Innes hesitated. She had been hoping that Meg would go with her, but second thoughts made her cautious. Women on their own were very vulnerable on the highway, even if they looked like beggars. And if they were carrying a box of valuables, they could easily be murdered for that alone. In addition there would be the added hazard of the garrison at Dundallon.

Bess Duncan had once told her that her dark red hair was a distinctive feature in her family, and suspicion could easily be aroused if they were questioned by the soldiers. But she and Thomas could look like any husband and wife travelling to new employment, with their poor belongings strapped to their backs.

For the first time Thomas Bell gazed at Innes with respect, his small tired eyes suddenly bright with interest and hope.

'I took the Lady Eleanor's strongbox of valuables,' Innes explained, 'to prevent it from falling into the hands of the scavengers.'

'Aye, and rightly, Mistress,' Thomas

approved, 'and you think it might contain gold?'

'I do not know for certain, Thomas, but it contains jewels and pearls to thread through the hair; but Meg says you would not be able to sell those.'

'I might be accused of beggary,' said Thomas, 'and have my cheek burned. The beggars know how to be rid of their precious goods, but if I approach the beggars, they will take the valuables and give me nothing . . . or next to nothing. I risk being accused of murder if someone has been done to death, and trials are of short duration now that Sir Archibald Frazer no longer holds court. I will say this for Sir Archibald, he was aye a fair man.'

Thomas was growing well disposed towards his former landlord.

'We will leave at dawn,' he said. 'How far is it, Mistress?'

Innes had little idea since she and Janet had travelled in the dark and had been brought to Leyburn in a different direction from Invernairn, but she did not want any more suspicion from Thomas.

'We will be there and back before . . . before noon,' she said, confidently.

'I will lend you my shawl,' Meg told her. 'Your cloak is too fine.'

'Thank you,' said Innes without argument, though the shabby, dirty shawl was not pleasant to wear about her head and shoulders. Nevertheless she recognised that she looked like any other poor woman traveller, except that most of them had small children clinging to their skirts and a baby wrapped tightly within the shawl.

'I will do my best for such people,' Innes vowed to herself, 'when . . . '

When? Her mind quickly returned to the present from a rosy, fanciful future, where her fortunes had been restored and she was living the life of a noble lady once more. But that life had gone for ever, she remembered. She herself was now one of the poor. There might be enough valuables in Eleanor's box to buy her comfort for some time, but how could she exchange the goods for food and clothing? She thought about Lizzie, and wondered if she would be willing to do it for her.

Thoughts of Lizzie were always mixed up with thoughts about Ruari Stewart. Her nights were often sleepless for a few hours as she wondered what was happening at Glenallyn. Had they been forced to fight Livingstone's men, and had Ruari survived such a battle? Innes knew that he was young and strong and full of courage, but his daring could easily put him in danger.

Yet Innes was sure that he had not been harmed. She would have felt it inside her heart . . . surely she would! . . . if Ruari had been wounded or . . . or killed. Her heart grew cold and sick at the thought. Sometimes she hated him for thinking so little of her that he would have given her to Alexander; then her heart would leap with love for him, and not hatred, so that she could only think of him with longing.

Yet his feelings for her were not likely to be warm with love now that Invernairn was in ruins again, and many of his servants killed or wounded. Innes had tried to find out news, but few packmen came near Leyburn since Meg had no money to spend on fripperies, and it was the packmen who carried most of the gossip, as they travelled about. Lady Eleanor had often been avid for gossip, and had bought laces and threads she did not need in order to listen to tales of what was happening in the town. Innes had felt herself almost buried alive at Leyburn, but conditions might now be bearable if only she could relieve the poverty of the place.

Eagerness lent strength to her tired feet as she and Thomas walked further and further along the road towards Dundallon.

The morning had been cold and grey when they left Leyburn, but soon in the eastern sky a mist of pale greyish-pink lit the clouds, and the earth around them seemed to throb into life with the birth of a new day. Innes looked up at the great spears of fire which lit the sky, like jewels which were so much more beautiful than the ones she sought in Eleanor's strongbox, and her heart rose in expectation of the life that lay ahead. She was young and strong and full of hope. She was helping Meg to make cheese from the goat's milk, and to rear chickens on gleanings of grain. Soon Thomas and Meg would have renewed strength in their limbs, and would dig their daily plot with energy, so that the land would become productive once more, and they could buy an ox and a plough.

Her own future might be bleak, but she would make Meg and her family her own. She could look after Janet, and put clean rushes on the floor and drapes on the walls . . .

'Oh, Thomas, is not the dawn of a new day exciting?' she asked.

'It is like another yoke gripping my shoulders, Mistress,' said Thomas tiredly. 'Another day to be endured.'

Something in his tone angered her.

Ruari might have been as full of cares as Thomas Bell at one time when he had to start to rebuild Invernairn and had the responsibility of a great many men, women and children on his shoulders. But he had spent little time in sighing over what might have been. He had settled those servants who did not wish to remain at Invernairn, and banded together those who did. And when they had nothing to fill their bellies, he had gone out and begged in order to keep them alive, and start to rebuild.

'There are those who would envy you your lot, Thomas Bell,' she said, sharply. 'You have not been wounded grievously, and you are a free man and cannot be sold according to custom. Your wife works to your back, and your children do not sicken in spite of poor meat. If you tried harder you could be comfortable one day with a fine farm of rich pastures.'

'You have seen how we live, Mistress,' he said, sourly. 'It is not the castle.'

'No, but the castle was kept neat and trim on hard work. Perhaps, when we find my strongbox, there might be enough coins to give us a new start, Thomas Bell; but I will have the coins spent wisely and not on strong ale.'

'You have much to say for yourself this morning, Mistress,' said Thomas. The Lady had been silent of late, living within herself and pondering on how to make life more pleasant, as Meg had explained.

'I have,' she agreed, looking up at the sky which had grown pale grey once more, though she could see the storm clouds gathering from beyond the mountains. 'We had better hurry, Thomas,' she said, pulling Meg's shawl closer. 'The skies are growing leaden.'

'You will not melt, Mistress,' said Thomas, sulkily.

'But you might, Thomas,' said Innes, sweetly, 'then what should I do?'

'Cover me with leaves,' he returned with an attempt at humour so that she laughed. The sound was quite startling to her, and she realised that it was some time since her heart had been light enough for laughter.

Suddenly Thomas drew her into the side of the road as a party of horsemen rode in behind them and a henchman galloped up to clear the narrow path.

'Make way there,' he cried. 'Clear the highway.'

'Who asks?' demanded Thomas, surly because he had splashed into a puddle thick with mud.

'Would you quarrel wi' Sir Ruari Stewart of Glenallyn?' the henchman asked, and even as Innes almost gasped aloud with shock while her heart raced in her breast, the horsemen were upon them, riding swiftly in the direction of Invernairn. Innes' eyes were on the leader who was heavily clad in thick leather against the cold, seeing that he looked stern-faced with his mouth set in grim lines. For a moment it seemed that his eyes swept over her, but there was no recognition in them, and the party of horsemen galloped past with the henchman taking his place amongst them.

'Some day they will find a way to take the air from our lungs,' growled Thomas. 'How much further, Mistress?'

Innes hardly heard the question. She was weak and trembling with the shock of seeing Ruari again after thinking about him so much. And the henchman had referred to him as *Sir* Ruari Stewart of *Glenallyn*. What could that mean? could it be that Sir Alexander was dead, and that Ruari had inherited Glenallyn? If so, he would now be one of the greater barons in the land, and it was little wonder that his eyes had flickered over her without recognition. She looked down at her tattered clothing and worn shawl, and she felt very much like the beggar maid who had accompanied Lizzie and old Hannah Munro to beg from travellers all those weeks ago.

'Are we near that stream?' Thomas asked again, 'or is this some ploy of your own, Mistress? I warn ye, I'm no in a mood for these kind o' games.'

He shook her arm, and she freed herself with quiet dignity.

'Leave me be, Thomas Bell,' she said, haughtily so that he fell back a little.

'I'm sorry, Mistress, but we appear to walk further than you told me.'

'We have rounded the wood from a different direction,' said Innes, 'but here, now, is the stream and further there is the bend where I concealed the box.'

Thomas helped her to reach into the recess hollowed out by the stream. It looked just the same as it had been when she and Janet stood on this very spot, but there was nothing in the recess. Innes began to claw at the hole where she had buried the box and for a while she worked steadily, then she looked at Thomas with a white face.

'Help me to uncover this part, Thomas,' she said. 'This was the hiding place, but . . . '

Thomas worked beside her feverishly, but even as they groped around the recess, Innes' heart began to grow heavy. It was useless to look further. The strongbox had gone.

'Are you sure it was here?' Thomas was asking. 'We will skirt the woods and maybe we will see another part of the stream so like this one . . . '

'It was here, Thomas,' said Innes, dully. 'Look, you can see where the box rested. There are marks on the soil.'

Thomas looked and had to acknowledge that this was so, but his temper grew surly again with disappointment, and his respect for Innes diminished accordingly.

'Stupid females,' he muttered to himself. 'There would be a track left as clear to read as the target board.'

'Nay, Thomas, we took precautions, Janet and I,' said Innes. 'We did not disturb anything other than the hiding place.'

'Wi' ten pairs o' e'en watching you,' said Thomas bitterly. 'I should know better than listen to a female and have my hopes of easement raised.'

'Aye, you are always thinking of your easement,' flashed Innes. 'If you worked to your own benefit, you would have no need of anyone's gold coins. You would earn plenty of your own.'

'Not with extra mouths to feed,' Thomas grumbled. 'First, Janet Balfour and now you, Mistress, and de'il the hope o' your being restored to favour. De'il the thanks for hiding ye.'

'So you would be selling me to the soldiers now,' said Innes, scornfully.

She was beginning to have a reaction from seeing Ruari Stewart riding past in all his pride and glory, whilst she dragged her skirts in the mud. She felt she did not care very much what happened to her now.

'Go on then,' she urged. 'Go to Dundallon and tell them you have had a Frazer under your roof this past few weeks, and see if they give you gold for me, or have their swords at your throat for not reporting my presence to them before.'

Thomas went pale. 'I . . . I meant

nothing, Mistress,' he muttered. 'You were Janet's charge, and she is flesh and blood to my wife and children. Do you think I would betray you when it would rebound on my own flesh and blood? Nay, but it is hard for a poor man.'

'I am working for you, Thomas Bell,' said Innes. 'I have made cheese and put the hens on their lay. I have helped to look after your children so that your wife can work to your back. I have taken nothing from you which I have not repaid. I am sorry the strongbox has gone, but it was there . . . '

Who could have stolen it? she wondered, then her breath caught again as she realised the answer to that problem. It was Ruari Stewart, of course. She and Janet had been captured fairly near to this place. The beggars would no doubt have searched it next day to see if anything had been dropped, since they were carrying many bundles and they would have been led to the hiding place. Perhaps they had left marks on the soil, or her skirt had caught on a bramble bush and she had pulled it clear, perhaps leaving threads caught. Her hands had been soiled with earth when she was brought to Invernairn too. It would not be difficult for Ruari, the beggar lord, to put two and two together.

So he had kept her valuables, she thought bitterly, her heart heavy with pain, and he had not come to find her at Leyburn. If he were the Master of Glenallyn, he could have found somewhere for her to stay, with enough substance from her own monies to feed and clothe her. He would have known the strongbox belonged to her, because their coat of arms was stamped upon it; so it was no excuse to plead that the box had merely been found and no owner traced. He had more or less stolen it from her, thought Innes, the slow anger gradually mounting, so that she walked faster and faster.

The sky had grown leaden, and, as the wind dropped, the heavy rain began to come on and to soak into their clothing. Thomas' temper grew even more evil, and by the time they arrived back at Leyburn and Meg met them eagerly outside the door of the farmstead, he thrust her out of the way with a blow which felled her to the ground.

'How dare you take out your ill-temper on poor Meg,' cried Innes, and for a moment she thought that she, too, would receive another such blow, and his face was twisted with rage and hatred.

'The nobles!' he said, scathingly. 'Wha can depend on the nobles?'

'Try learning to depend on yourself,' she flung at him, then bit her lip from saying more when she saw that the children had gathered and were looking at them with frightened faces. Meg had paid one or two extra visits to the well, and they had been washed and their hair had a semblance of tidiness.

Innes had dropped on her knees beside Meg who moaned a little.

'Bring water,' she said to the eldest boy.

Thomas had gone into one of the out-buildings, and the child obeyed her. She wiped Meg's face and forced her to drink a little.

'The gold coins?' whispered Meg.

'Gone . . . the box had gone,' said Innes, whilst Meg moaned again. 'Do not be frightened, Meg,' Innes promised her. 'I will help you somehow. Somehow I will find coins for you to buy food and . . . and an ox, and to pay for a servant. Thomas Bell will not hurt you again.'

'It is nothing,' said Meg, and Innes knew that the blow had not been the first.

She went into the farmstead and stared at Janet, going over to talk to the old woman who was fast becoming bedridden.

'Janet!' she said, urgently, 'do you remember how we hid the box? Were the beggars nearby? Did you hear a sound?'

Janet looked at her without recognition and Innes sighed. The only things she was sure about was that Ruari Stewart had taken her strongbox.

9

For a few days Innes worked like a demon, making cheese, collecting and washing eggs and trying to make sweet-meats from the wild honey they had collected, which could be exchanged for other goods.

She had visited many farms with Archibald when she was growing up, and now she tried to remember how the women of the well-run prosperous farms spent their time. She collected wool and dyed it with leaves, but found difficulty in spinning and weaving it to make garments for the children and she tried to recover Janet's 'treasures' . . . her own gowns . . . to dye them and make them fit Meg and herself, but Janet held on to the bundle with fierce strength, and Innes only succeeded in stealing back one gown which she dyed for Meg. But Meg was too large-boned for the gown and, with inward relief, Innes exchanged her tattered gown for the new one.

Then one day she had a visitor. Meg saw a small party of men and women coming along the moorland path and she drew in her breath with annoyance.

'It's beggars,' she said. 'They will want food and a night's lodging, and they never believe we cannot give them meat. Thomas says we can expect gangs of them now wi' the country becoming so lawless.'

Innes nodded. The lack of a strong hand on the country's affairs was beginning to be felt, and nobles did not regard Regent Douglas as being someone to be obeyed. The quarrels meant that more and more poor people were taking to the road, and travellers abroad were being surrounded by beggars asking for alms.

'They are better off than those from whom they beg,' said Innes, looking at Meg's tattered state. 'I will send them away, Meg, never fear.'

'No, Mistress!' cried Meg. 'They will be able to tell you are no maidservant. Your tongue reveals that you have learning, and the beggars are used to summing up their victims.'

Nevertheless, Innes hung in the background when Meg went to the door to confront the beggars, and Innes caught her breath when she recognised Lizzie and one of the older women from Invernairn. They were accompanied by a thin elderly man and a tall, strong fellow who had lost an arm. Innes recognised Robert Cowden who had ridden with Ruari.

'What are ye wanting wi' me and mine?' Meg was demanding.

'Food and shelter,' Lizzie told her, boldly, 'for me and my man, and our friends.'

'So you have come to Leyburn,' said Innes, stepping forward. 'You must know that Thomas and Meg Bell have to feed their children and Meg's mother . . .'

'Not forgetting yourself, Mistress

Frazer,' said Lizzie, her eyes gleaming as they ran over Innes' changed appearance. 'How do you fare as a servant maid, Mistress Innes?'

'Well enough, Lizzie. Is your mother well?'

The beggars had practically forced their way into the farmstead, and seemed glad to sit down in the warmth. The continued rain had turned the roads into quagmires, though the countryside was as fresh and green as emeralds. Even Thomas was heartened to see that grass and crops were growing in the soil, that he had begun to tend daily.

Lizzie stared at Janet Balfour who looked back at her with a blank stare.

'My mother is dead,' she said, her voice hard and flat. 'She sickened after Invernairn was burned.'

Again her eyes turned to Innes.

'The master was lookin' for ye, Mistress. Ye can thank my Uncle Will and me that he did not find ye. He was in a fine boiling anger and he would have run ye through himself, I'll swear, if he had found ye at Invernairn.'

Innes sank to her knees beside the fire so that she would stop trembling.

'So he was in a rage?' she asked.

'Aye, a terrible rage, but he has money now and Invernairn is being built up again; and this time it will not be easy to burn. This time, though, I am not waiting to be roasted in my bed. My mother is dead and I have left Invernairn. We have joined the beggars.'

'Oh no, Lizzie!' cried Innes. 'You should not be a beggar.' She glanced at Robert Cowden.

'Are you wed?' she asked.

Lizzie shrugged. 'We have not paid fees to the priest, but we declared ourselves wed before Hannah and Andrew Meikle, these friends you see before you. We are as wed as we will ever be and we go beggaring. Robert has lost his arm in battle. How can he earn his living wi' honest toil? He canna fight and he canna dig his plot.'

'He looks as strong as my own man,'

said Meg. 'We hae no meat for beggars.'

'I heard that Master Stewart was now Sir Ruari,' said Innes, hoping to avoid argument, and eager for news.

'Aye. Sir Alexander's wounds had an eye of evil hanging over them and they went black as the De'il himself. Sir Ruari fought off Livingstone's men and they went back to Stirling where the Queen resides with the King under the protection of Livingstone. When Sir Alexander died, Master Ruari claimed Glenallyn, since he was the heir. He rides between Glenallyn and Invernairn, with his Lady . . . '

'His Lady!' cried Innes and did not know that her eyes grew black with pain. 'What Lady?'

'Lady Mary Stewart . . . Mistress Mary Hamilton that was, and now Lady Stewart. Have ye heard no news, Mistress?'

Innes shook her head. She saw Lizzie looking at her with a malicious smile on her lips.

'It was a mistake to encourage James

Livingstone, Mistress,' she said. 'It has brought grief to innocent people.'

'I did *not* encourage him,' cried Innes, colour staining her cheeks. 'I hate him.'

'And he hates you, as I've heard. His face has been made hideous with your burning torch. If his chieftain, Sir Alexander, had not ordered him to help man the garrison at Stirling, he would have scoured the country for you. He says he can wait, and he will pluck you from the tree like ripened fruit. I wonder who will find ye first, Mistress . . . Sir Ruari, or Master James?'

Innes felt as though her heart had been filled with ice. She had had nightmares about James Livingstone, and her loathing of him had caused her to cry out in the night. Her thoughts went to Sir Ruari and to her glimpse of his hard cold face. He would have no mercy either. He was blaming her for destroying Invernairn which had been restored with such difficulty, and how he must hate her! And his wife?

. . . Lady Mary Stewart?

'What is she like?' she asked Lizzie.

'Who?'

'Lady Mary Stewart.'

Lizzie leaned forward. 'She is as beautiful as a dream. Come now, Mistress, we will hae wheaten cake and cheese if ye have no meat.'

'I will find ye something,' said Meg, sourly, 'but my man will not be pleased. And ye can sleep in the barn, if ye will. There is nae room ben the house.'

'Stop yer whining!' said Lizzie, rather wearily. 'We hae brought ye meat, enough for us all, and even if I have no love for Mistress Innes since she helped to finish my mother . . . '

Innes drew back with a small cry.

' . . . Oh aye, ye did,' Lizzie insisted, 'even if ye did not squeeze the life from her yourself; but Will Munro bade us come, and says to hide yourself, Mistress. Ye are sought from all quarters. The master seeks ye constantly, with blackness in his heart, and so does Livingstone, and the Queen's men. Remain here. That's all I can say.'

Innes nodded. 'Thank you, Lizzie,' she managed.

The news was far from good, but most of all was Ruari's search for her in the heat of anger, and . . . and his wife . . . his wife . . .

Innes pretended that the smoke had blown into her face as she forced down a sob.

'The bairn is weeping, Lady Eleanor,' said Janet in a loud voice, so that they all looked round, startled. 'Hide, my lass, hide!' she cried.

'She is raving,' said Lizzie.

This time Innes made no attempt to stop her tears.

★ ★ ★

A week later Will Munro headed a small party of horsemen who rode up to Leyburn. Meg had bidden Innes hide in a small recess which they had prepared, in the event that Leyburn would be searched by the soldiers, and she crawled into this tight corner, scarcely able to breathe.

'It is Will Munro!' Meg called as the horsemen reined in. 'How do you say, Mistress? Are ye still in hiding?'

'No, I will see Will Munro,' said Innes. 'He means me no harm. It was he who brought me here to safety.'

'I doubt if it is safe ye are now,' muttered Meg darkly. 'Thomas is more and more evil-tempered after the loss o' yer strongbox, Mistress. I have been afraid he would tell the soldiers in the hopes o' reward. Maybe we had better be careful.'

'It is little use trying to tell Will Munro that I am not here,' said Innes, wearily.

She had noticed that Meg was ill-at-ease and nervous, and often scanned the horizon, and now the reason was made clear. She could no longer depend upon Leyburn as a haven.

Innes went to the door to greet Will, who came forward to meet her slowly and rather ponderously.

'Greetings, Will,' she smiled. 'I see you are in good health.'

'And you, Mistress,' he returned. The fresh air and healthy exercise, together with the good cheese and wheaten cake was beginning to bring a fine healthy glow to Innes' cheeks.

'Do you ride to Stirling?' she asked. 'I have heard the Queen is in residence there.'

'Under lock and key more like,' grunted Will, He stared hard at Innes. 'Pack yer belongings, Mistress Innes, and we will be on our way.'

Her face paled. 'Where to, Will?'

'Glenallyn,' he said, briefly. 'Sir Ruari knows that you are here, and he demands that you be taken to Glenallyn without delay.'

'You told him, Will?'

'Not I!' he denied. 'He was in such a rage when Livingstone attacked Inver-nairn and when he found out the reason for it, that no man dare mention your name. I am sorry, Mistress,' he said in a low voice. 'Those two beggars, the Meikles, informed on you, hoping for reward. Now ye go to Glenallyn.'

'We gave them food and shelter,' cried Meg, 'and now they would harm the young Mistress.'

She was distressed now that Innes was leaving, and as she looked round her home she realised that the girl had transformed it for her. Her energy and enthusiasm had forced her and Thomas to work a little harder, so that they were producing more, and the home was a sweeter place to live in. The children were cleaner and more obedient and they had been taught a small amount of learning, which they would not have had if Mistress Innes had not come to live with them. She had even helped to look after old Janet whose eyes were now completely blank.

'What will happen to me, Will?' asked Innes.

Will shook his head. 'There are no orders, ma'am, but that you are to pack yer belongings and come with us.'

'Belongings!' cried Innes. 'They will be easily packed. Anything of value which I possessed is already at Glenallyn!'

Meg found her cloak and wrapped it round Innes shoulders, and suddenly hugged the girl to her.

'Goodbye, Mistress. God go with you.'

'I will come again, Meg, if I can,' Innes promised.

Meg nodded and wiped a tear with the corner of her apron. Will helped the girl to mount the horse which had been brought for her, and she pulled the cloak closer around her. She felt sick with dread at the thought of the ride to Glenallyn, then her heart leapt jerkily. She would see Ruari again, even if he would smite her down in his rage. Could he not see that the destruction of Invernairn had been none of her doing?

'Has there been fighting with Livingstone, Will?' she asked.

'Aye, Mistress. Sir Ruari taught James Livingstone a sharp lesson when he heard that Livingstone was riding to Roxburgh. Livingstone turned tail for Stirling, but he is an ill man to cross. He will be back at Glenallyn before the snaws are on the ground.'

'That might be soon, Will,' said Innes, shivering, though she was probably chilled more in heart than body.

'Is . . . is Lady Mary Stewart at Glenallyn, Will?' she asked.

'Aye with her sister, Mistress Jane Hamilton.'

Innes heaved a deep sigh. She had never met the Hamiltons and could expect no help from them. Was Lady Mary wearing any of Eleanor's jewels? she wondered. Or perhaps they were not good enough for my Lady Stewart. Innes' small chin firmed as she rode beside Will. If they looked down their noses at her, she would not care. She was as wellborn as any Hamilton.

10

The beauty of Glenallyn again caught at Innes' heart as they rode into the courtyard of the old castle, and she was handed down to stand stiffly beside her mount before it was led away to be fed and watered.

'This way, Mistress,' said Will, but Innes was already moving towards the main entrance. A moment later the courtyard seemed to swarm with men and women, then Ruari Stewart strode forward and Innes was looking up into his face.

She saw that his eyes were blazing with a strange light as he stepped forward, while others made way for him.

'Well ... Mistress Innes,' he said, very softly, 'so you are here at last. I thought never to see you again.'

'I am here, *Sir* Ruari,' she replied and

he smiled faintly, then his eyes swept over her, taking in every detail of her appearance.

'A beggar maid once more I see,' he said. 'As you once told me, there are those who begin to enjoy the life.' His eyes gleamed again with the devil in them.

'It was none of my choice, sir!' she cried.

'Nevertheless I cannot talk to you while you pollute the air with your odours.'

'Your own were just as offensive,' she said, harshly, 'as I remember.'

Again she caught a gleam in his eyes as he looked around him.

'You . . . Annie Hall . . . take Mistress Frazer to her room, and see that she is made clean. She is to be brought to the great hall when she is ready.'

'Aye, Sir Ruari,' said the girl, bobbing a curtsey. 'Would ye come wi' me, Mistress?'

'I know the way,' said Innes. She felt humiliated beyond anything, but she was also apprehensive about the way Ruari intended to deal with her. She had seen the devilish look in his eyes before, and it boded ill for someone. This time it appeared that she was on the receiving end.

⋆   ⋆   ⋆

The water was deliciously warm and scented with rose petals, and Annie Hall spent a long time in making sure that Innes was as clean as the day she was born. Helping at Leyburn had taken its toll on her hands and fingernails, and her beautiful long dark red hair had become slightly tangled with lack of facilities for keeping it well-groomed. Innes had shrieked more than once as Annie tugged at her curls, but Annie had been given her orders and none dare disobey the master!

Another maidservant, Sarah Laidlaw, had made up the fire in the bedchamber, and Innes began to look round whilst Annie dried her soft skin, now slightly pink here and there where she had been scrubbed with vigour.

'This is not the bedchamber I was given last time,' she remarked, seeing that it was, perhaps, bigger and even more opulent than the other.

'No, ma'am,' said Anne. 'Mistress Jane Hamilton occupies your old apartment.'

'Oh. And Lady Mary Stewart?'

'She occupies the main chamber since she . . . '

'I understand,' Innes said, quickly. Lady Mary was mistress of the household.

Annie picked up some underclothing, and helped Innes to dress. They were some of her own garments which had been left behind, since she had been too disturbed to remember everything. Then the girl disappeared behind a screen and returned with the most beautiful gown Innes had ever seen. It was in heavy cream silk encrusted with pearls, and there was a matching silk band to be placed, like a coronet, round her head. It was the sort of gown the Queen might have worn had she not been in mourning.

'That is not mine,' she said, sharply.

Annie hesitated. 'No, ma'am, but Lady Mary and Mistress Jane helped to alter it for you.'

The blood mounted in Innes' cheeks. 'I will not wear a gown other than my own,' she said.

'But . . . Mistress Innes . . . ' The maidservant looked horror-stricken. 'Your gown is . . . is soiled . . . '

'It can be washed and dried by the fire.'

'But Sir Ruari . . . '

'If you bring my cloak, I will see Sir Ruari and tell him I only wear my own gowns. The others are now lost to me, but if I am to stay here for any length of time, I can no doubt arrange with Sir Ruari to have others made; but I do not wear other people's gowns.'

'Aye, Mistress,' said the girl, sullenly.

Innes was left by the fireside whilst Annie handed her gown to Sarah

Laidlaw. It was to be washed in the laundryroom and dried by the huge fires. The sewing woman mended the tears, but compared with the lovely silk gown, it was a drab thing when it was returned to her.

Nevertheless after weeks of rags and tatters, Innes felt fresh and neat when the gown was pulled over her petticoats and tied into place. Annie had found a ribbon and dressed her hair, which now fell in a cascade of curls to her waist.

'Well? Am I not neat and clean?' she asked Annie.

'Aye, Mistress, but Sir Ruari gave his orders. I fear I will have displeased him.'

'I will tell him I would have no other,' Innes assured her. 'I am entitled to choose my own gown.'

'Aye, Mistress,' said Annie, doubtfully.

'Where is Marjorie the housekeeper?' Innes asked.

'Dead of the fever,' Annie replied, tonelessly. 'Lady Mary became mistress of the castle.'

There were several people gathered in the great hall when Innes walked along the corridor and down the steps which led from the private apartments, and Ruari detached himself from the group and came forward to greet her. Innes was aware of a great hush in the conversation, and she saw that the Ladies had turned to stare at her.

'Now I can recognise Mistress Innes,' said Ruari, though almost immediately his eyes grew brilliant and sparkled like diamonds as they swept over her.

'What is this? Where is your gown?'

'This is the only gown I possess,' said Innes, clearly. 'I have no other, and I will wear none other than my own.'

For a long moment they measured one another, then he threw back his head and laughed.

'Very well, if you wish to go to your wedding in rags, so be it. It will be none the less legal.'

'My . . . my wedding!' she cried, stupidly.

'You are a great nuisance to me,

Mistress Innes,' he told her, and she could see that his eyes were glittering again. 'You need the protection of a husband, so I have arranged for the priest to marry us in the chapel next to the great hall. Afterwards there will be merry-making, because a wedding is a merry occasion. My cousin, Lady Mary Stewart, and her sister, Mistress Jane will witness the marriage along with my good friend, Sir Donald Gordon.'

'But . . . I cannot marry you!' she cried. 'What do you mean?'

Her head felt ready to burst with shock as he pulled her to one side of the room.

'Aye, that you can,' he told her, holding her arm like a vice. 'This time I will not have tantrums. You will marry me and be done with it. You repulsed Alexander, but he found a fine wife in Lady Mary . . . '

'Sir Alexander's wife?'

'Aye, poor lady. There was no live child born to her and no time to make other children. But we'll have time,

Mistress Innes. I will not lose you again.'

Her heart hammered at his words, and if they had been accompanied by tenderness, she would have surged with happiness; but Ruari's face was white, and it seemed that she was witnessing the great rage which both Lizzie and Will had mentioned. She grew cold with fear again.

'You cannot marry me,' she gasped. 'I am sought by the soldiers. The Queen knows who I am, and she will be enraged that a sister of the King's murderers dared to attend the princesses. Her rage will reach out to you.'

'The Queen is in Stirling,' he told her. 'She was imprisoned by Livingstone until she signed over the guardianship of the King. Livingstone thinks that he holds the power if he holds the King. Douglas is a sick man, and his heir is little more than a boy. The Queen has enough troubles of her own and will have no time to worry about you. Besides . . . I hope to do her a service . . . '

'How?'

'By aiding Crichton. He is a friend to the Queen, and I know how we can return the King to his care. I have a plan. The Queen will be grateful, and will not frown upon my wife so long as she is a Lady born . . . '

'I should have thought that Mistress Jane . . . '

The light left his eyes. 'Will marry Sir Donald Gordon in a few weeks. You make many difficulties, Ma'am.'

'You thrust it upon me,' she said, goaded.

If only he had shown that he held her in affection, but it seemed that he had a conscience about her. He had captured her, then tried to marry her to Glenallyn, and now he would protect her himself. But protection was not love, and her heart craved for love.

'Will ye run to Stirling now?' he asked, scathingly, 'and become a nurse-maid once more? Why cannot you be a nursemaid to your own children?'

She went scarlet.

'Come on, Ma'am. There is no time, and you are as slippery as an eel. Lady Mary and Mistress Jane made you a wedding gown but it does not suit such a proud female. You must come to me in rags. Well, if you prefer rags, then that is what you may have; but you keep your guests waiting. I have promised feasting and merry-making, and our guests will want to enjoy it, even if we do not.'

'Very well, Sir Ruari,' said Innes, meekly.

Suddenly she was wildly happy, whatever the circumstances.

★   ★   ★

The cool look in Lady Mary's eyes when she saw that Innes was not wearing the gown, warned Innes that she had made an enemy.

Ruari introduced her to the two ladies and Sir Donald, and Innes curtseyed prettily to them, though she was now feeling very conscious that her gown was far from becoming, and that all three were staring at her with unashamed curiosity.

'Mistress Innes dislikes borrowed plumes,' Ruari said, easily. 'She goes to her wedding like a scarecrow, but I dare say that the priest will mumble the same vows over us whatever she wears.'

'Perhaps it would be expedient to postpone your marriage for one or two more days,' said Lady Mary, sweetly, 'and give Mistress Frazer time to have her own bridal gown made to her taste.'

She smiled at Ruari, but as her eyes met Innes', the girl knew that Lady Mary was inwardly enraged about the proposed match. The widow wanted Ruari for herself, thought Innes, and it must have caused her a few pangs to alter the silk gown for her. No doubt Lady Mary would have had a few sly remarks to make, calculated to take all the pleasure from her wedding had Innes worn it.

But now Ruari was shaking his head and laughing, his fingers gripping

Innes' arm. 'I have little time to spare for such niceties,' he told them. 'I must be about the King's business. The priest is here, and we have guests and meat and wine for celebrations. We will have music and dancing, and all that is missing is a bridal gown. Mistress Innes is happy to wear her own feathers, and if she is happy, why then, so am I!'

Again there was the faintest pressure on her arm, but Innes' eyes were on Lady Mary whose rather petulant mouth had hardened.

Jane Hamilton, on the other hand, smiled at her kindly, and Innes knew whose needle had stitched at the pretty silk gown.

'Would you allow me to give you a wedding gift, Mistress Innes?' she asked, shyly. 'My own wedding is near and I have had time to prepare for it. Sir Donald has recently returned from France and is busy about his estate, so we arrange our wedding shortly.'

Innes was touched by the offer which was delicately made.

'I . . . I had no thought of wedding gifts,' she said. 'I . . . ' Again she felt the light pressure. 'I would be honoured to accept.'

'It is merely a shawl,' said Jane, and produced a beautiful cream silk shawl which she draped over Innes' shoulders, so that her long dark red hair suddenly came to life. Warmth touched Innes' skin, and her eyes shone, brilliant as liquid gold, so that Jane smiled with admiration.

'You look very beautiful, ma'am,' she said.

Lady Mary's eyes darted venomously at her sister, but she was obliged to turn and echo the remarks. Innes had no doubt about accepting the gift.

'Why it is as fine as any bridal gown,' she said. 'Do you not think so, Sir Ruari?'

'We waste time,' he said, seeing that the priest was restless, having other duties to perform. 'You look very well, ma'am.'

Often Innes had tried to picture her

own wedding when she was a young girl at Dundallon, and was dreaming about her future. Always her bridegroom had been handsome, with herself in silks and jewels; but never could she have pictured the bizarre marriage which took place in the small chapel at Glenallyn. She pulled the shawl close about her shoulders, and made her responses in a colourless voice, very much aware of the tall, hard man who stood beside her. She was making her promises before God, and hoped she would still the fear in her heart.

And what of Ruari Stewart? Did he, too, fear and love God before whom he also gave his promises? Why had he chosen her and not Lady Mary? He treated the other woman like a close relative, but he must know that there could be no barrier to such a marriage if he had desired it. Lady Mary would have been willing.

Innes knelt for the blessing, and again Ruari's hand was on her arm as he guided her back to the great hall where everyone had gathered for feasting and merry-making. Now she felt inexpressibly tired, and could scarcely remember lying a-bed in restful sleep. It seemed a long time since early morning when Will had come for her. Her bones ached wearily and the music and dancing resounded in her head.

Ruari had put himself into a roistering mood, and was loud in his exhortations for everyone to enjoy themselves and to eat and drink their fill.

'Come, wife, we must enjoy our celebrations. We will dance and sing and listen to the music.'

'No, I . . . '

'What ails you, Lady Innes?'

She looked up at him white-faced. 'I am very tired, sir. It . . . it has been a long ride from Leyburn.'

'Then we leave our guests to the celebrations and we retire,' he informed her. 'Where is Annie Hall? She will attend you. Lady Mary will see to our guests.'

Innes' legs felt like cotton wool when

she was conducted to the bridal chamber, where a fire burned brightly, and Annie Hall hurried in to disrobe the new Lady Innes.

'Leave me be,' said Innes, sitting down by the fireside. 'Loosen my stays and I will disrobe myself.'

Her nerves were raw, and she felt she would scream if she received any more attention that night.

Sir Ruari was still downstairs, laughing with his guests, and she wondered if he would begin to drink wine and would not trouble her that night. She could hear the noise of revelry, but now it was faint, and after a while she felt less exhausted and began to remove her garments. The shawl she laid out lovingly on a chest. It was very beautiful and Innes suspected that it had been brought in from France. She was grateful to Jane Hamilton, and felt that they could be friends but for Lady Mary.

Innes disrobed, until she was standing in her shift, then she slipped into the huge bed. She had no bed gown but she was too tired to care. A second later she was wide awake as the door was thrust open and Sir Ruari walked in.

'My bride is a-bed,' he said, happily. 'So much the better.'

'Sir . . . you do not intend to . . . to . . . '

She paled as she realised that Ruari was far from being fatigued as she was herself. The bridal chamber was the master bedroom, and Innes began to panic as she realised the import of this. It was going to be her new bedchamber while she lived at Glenallyn, and already she was finding the sombre furnishings oppressive.

Ruari came over to the bed to stand beside her, but as he reached out to stroke her hair, she shrank away so that his eyes began to gleam with the fierce light she had come to know so well.

'What's this?'

His fingers encountered the soft white linen of a bedgown which had been laid for Innes at the foot of the bed. She had not noticed it.

'You do not even deign to wear your bedgown? It seems that we have nothing good enough for you, Lady Innes.'

She looked at the anger in his eyes, and her own was stirred.

'Or could it be that you prefer to come to me . . . without your bedgown?'

She choked back her fury. 'Perhaps you should have allowed me to wear my sister's jewels . . . those belonging to the Lady Eleanor Frazer,' she said, proudly.

He had snuffed the candles, and she saw his dark shape for a second, silhouetted against the firelight, before he climbed into bed.

'You can wear what you wish, my Lady. I find your sweet body the most precious jewel.'

'Great heavens, Sir, you waste no time,' panted Innes, though her own heart raced to match his.

'I have waited too long already,' said Ruari.

'And you feel that you must have an

heir,' said Innes, 'as I remember.'

He chuckled and kissed her. 'It seems I have captured my bird,' he said, with satisfaction, 'with or without jewels.'

'You have the jewels,' she cried. If only he would take her in his arms and tell her he loved her, how sweet this night might be. She felt suffocated by his nearness, but she would not own to love when he did not ask it of her. She was just a young, healthy woman of good family who was going to bear his children, but she could not forget that he had stolen from her.

'You shall have your jewels tomorrow,' he promised. Then his voice grew cooler. 'It would seem that you are like other women after all, more concerned with jewels than . . . than pleasure.'

'You are the one who seeks pleasure,' she cried, and he stiffened beside her.

'So my captured bird intends to sing only when it would have seed,' said Ruari. He had pulled her into his arms again, exploring her body with obvious delight, but now he pushed her away.

'Go to sleep then, Lady Innes. I think I will make sure that the castle is secure.'

She heard him pulling on his garments once more, and a moment later the door of the chamber closed behind him. Innes was too tired and drained even to weep, but tomorrow Ruari had promised to return her jewels, and she might sell them for coins. She thought about Meg and of the hard aching life she had left behind. But physical weariness was as nothing to the weariness of her emotions bound up as they were in someone else who did not care deeply enough for her.

★   ★   ★

Annie Hall came into the bedchamber the following morning, looking at Innes curiously. Already she must know that Sir Ruari had not spent the night in the bridal chamber, and must wonder if she had not pleased her bridegroom. There was evidence that she had not repulsed him either, thought Innes, with red-dened cheeks.

'Mistress Jane wishes to know if she can lend you a morning gown, my Lady,' said Annie, bobbing a curtsey.

'Thank her, but I will wear my own,' said Innes, her pride up in arms once more. When Ruari produced her strongbox she would have money with which to purchase new gowns. It did not occur to her that Sir Ruari would now be responsible for her daily needs.

'Yes, my Lady,' said Annie. 'Sir Ruari would see you in his business room when you have broken your fast. Will you have your meat served here, ma'am?'

'A small portion. I have no appetite,' said Innes. 'Are the guests still a-bed, Annie?'

'Some have ridden out early in the morning and have not rested in their bedchambers,' said Annie. 'The servants are making the great hall clean again before you are about, ma'am. Will you wish to see the kitchens, and to give

270

orders about the meals to be cooked?'

Innes remembered that she had not been welcome in the kitchens on the last occasion; then she realised that she was now mistress of Glenallyn. She would have to take up her new duties, and it would be up to her whether the castle was clean and well-run, or whether it gradually slipped into decline.

She remembered Lady Eleanor's lectures on this point, but that was so long ago that she could scarcely remember all that Lady Eleanor had taught her.

She looked at Annie who regarded her almost anxiously.

'I will look at all the kitchens and the store rooms,' she said, briskly, 'and I will wish to see how provisions are ordered and who is responsible for each task. Glenallyn is well run, as I remember, and I intend to keep it that way.'

'Aye, my Lady.'

Annie smiled and Innes could sense the relief in her. The servants liked a strong mistress who could make decisions and accept responsibility. Well, if Ruari had married her in order to secure the line, he would find that he had also acquired a mistress for his household, and one who liked discipline and obedience.

'I will see the sempstress as soon as possible,' she said, 'and have the new gowns made. Will you ask her to come to the sewing room in one hour, Annie?'

'Aye, my Lady,' the girl said, and Innes could hear the clatter of her feet on the stone corridor.

After eating her breakfast, Innes made her way to the business room to join Ruari. Sir Donald Gordon was already there, and both men were poring over maps, and discussing the fortifications at Stirling.

Sir Donald looked up with a smile when he saw Innes standing in the doorway, but there was no warmth in Ruari's eyes. He looked tired as though he had slept little the previous night, and his linen was crumpled. Neither she nor Ruari looked like a newly-wed pair, thought Innes, and a stranger would have been surprised had they been introduced as the Earl of Glenallyn and his Lady. She smiled a little at the thought, and Sir Donald bowed.

'I shall leave you for a moment, Sir Ruari,' he said. 'I know you must have things to discuss with the Lady Innes.'

He closed the heavy door gently, and Innes walked further into the room whilst Ruari continued to regard her silently.

'You look in a remarkably good humour, my Lady,' he said mockingly. 'Marriage must agree with you, or can it be the thought of those jewels you are so anxious to run through your fingers? It is a wonder you did not want to thread them through your hair before I bedded you.'

She went scarlet at his tone and her eyes glinted. 'Why not?' she asked, 'since they are my own.'

'They belong to the mistress of

Glenallyn,' he said, selecting a key from a safe box on the table. 'You are, of course, the mistress of Glenallyn, so they must, therefore, be your own. Please remember, however, that they will also belong to our son's wife, and the wife of our grandson. You are merely the custodian of these jewels.'

He had lifted a strongbox and turned the key in the lock, throwing open the lid. Innes gasped when she saw the gems which lay inside the box, and Ruari grasped her hand and draped necklaces and hair ornaments over her palm. Innes dropped them on to the table as though they were burning her.

'No!' she cried. 'I do not mean these jewels. These are yours, not mine. I would like you to return Lady Eleanor's strongbox.'

He frowned. 'I do not understand you.'

'It was gone from its hiding place, just beyond the spot where you captured Janet and me when . . . when we left Dundallon. You must have seen

274

us hiding it. There was no one else. It contained all Lady Eleanor's jewels, and even though they are not so fine as the Glenallyn jewels, they were quite fine enough. But more than that, I want to see if there are any gold coins in the box.'

He stared at her very coldly. 'You think I took this box from you?' he retorted heavily.

'Only for safe keeping,' she pleaded. 'Perhaps you have forgotten, Ruari? I did want the gold coins so very much.'

'And I do not steal,' he said, and his voice chilled her. 'I have begged my bread from those who could afford to spare me a little, and I have helped to share out riches from those who had more than enough. I do not take family treasures, however, and I only accept that which is freely given. I do not steal.'

'You took that which was not freely given last night,' she flung at him, and thought he was going to strike her. Instead he put the gems back into the box and locked them away; then he took a handful of gold coins from another strongbox and put them into her hand.

'I will have nothing but my own!' she cried. 'If you do not have my jewels then I . . . I apologise.'

'I have nothing of yours,' he said, very softly, ignoring her apology. 'I am also paying for what I had last night.'

She gasped and would have thrown the coins into his face if he had not caught her by the wrist. 'Take care or you will earn yourself a handful for your other hand,' he told her gently, and she almost screamed with rage. Now she could see that his glittering eyes had been bright with excitement.

'I will be leaving for Garloch to escort Lady Mary and Mistress Jane to their home,' he told her. 'Lady Mary will stay there until Craighall is ready for her. She does not wish to stay in Glenallyn now that it has a new mistress.'

'I do not know why you did not

marry her!' cried Innes. 'She wants you enough.'

'If she had wanted me, she could have had me,' said Ruari, cruelly, and the angry tears stung her eyes. 'I will be gone several days because I ride to Edinburgh from Garloch. I have business with Sir William Crichton. I leave Glenallyn well guarded and I expect you to take over as its mistress. I have no need to tell you your duties.'

'I seem to have fulfilled the principal one already.'

His lip curled. 'I deserve you for having no better judgment,' he declared almost to himself. 'A man can be a fool when it comes to a woman.'

She pulled at the heavy door but he was there before her, opening it with a courtly bow. Seconds later she was running along to her room, and it was only when she was shedding angry tears on the bed that she realised she was still clutching her gold coins. Some time he would have them back, she vowed; in the same fashion as he had given them to her. They would be returned with interest.

She could hear voices along the corridor and the high tinkle of laughter from Lady Mary. Innes rose to her feet, dashing the tears from her eyes with water which had been left for her in a large bowl. It had been scented with herbs, and she held them against her skin till it felt cool and fresh.

Carefully she put the coins away since she had earned them, her face disdainful as she dropped them into a box. If Sir Ruari thought that made her into his kept woman, then he would find out differently. So he might have married Lady Mary . . . if she had consented to have him. Well, he had not married Lady Mary. For some reason best known to himself, he had married her, and now they would all find out she was, indeed, the mistress of Glenallyn.

Smoothing her hair and her gown Innes walked downstairs towards the Great Hall. As she walked along the corridor, she looked into a small apartment used as a sewing room to see if the sempstress was waiting, but instead Jane Hamilton was there. The girl smiled at her, warmly.

'We will be riding home to Garloch today, Lady Innes,' she said. 'I must mend my riding cloak. I tore it on a branch when we rode to Glenallyn.'

'It had been a problem for me, too,' Innes laughed. 'I . . . er . . . I am sorry you leave so soon, Mistress Jane.' She looked at the other girl and thought that they might have been good friends if Jane had stayed longer. She was very grateful to the other girl for making her a gift of the lovely shawl. If only Ruari had had Eleanor's strongbox, she would have selected a pretty piece of jewellery for Jane. But she could see now that Ruari had not taken the box, and although she had tried to apologise to him, he had been in no mood to listen.

But if Ruari did not have it, then where had it gone? Had someone else been abroad that night, and watched her and Janet concealing the box? It had been dark, but perhaps they had been seen, and the hiding place investigated in daylight. At any rate, it was too late now.

She sighed a little as she sat down beside Jane.

'It is not fitting that my sister and I should stay, now that there is a new mistress in Glenallyn.'

'Your sister must feel that . . . that she has lost her home,' said Innes, beginning to see things from Lady Mary's point of view.

'She will have Craighall when it is ready. It is a fine home on the Glenallyn estate.'

'If she and Sir Alexander had had a son, this would always have been her home,' said Innes.

'She lost their child when news was brought that Sir Alexander was dead,' said Jane, and Innes' eyes widened. She would have had even more sympathy for Lady Mary had it not been for Ruari's parting remark.

'Oh . . . I . . . I am sorry,' she said awkwardly. 'I did not know. She cannot be feeling very happy having been widowed and made childless at a stroke.'

'She is young,' said Jane, 'and she has been well provided for by Sir Ruari. She may marry again. Rumour has it that the Queen is already thinking about taking another husband. Poor woman, she manages her affairs very ill on her own. They say she was practically kept in the dungeons at Stirling until she signed over the King to Livingstone.'

Innes shuddered. She could well believe it. 'I hope that did not last long,' she said.

'No, Sir Alexander Livingstone is now guardian of the King.'

'You stitch very well,' said Innes with admiration. 'I confess that I am ill-fitted to do fine work.'

'You have other talents, I am sure,' said Jane, 'and your sewing woman will not be displeased.' Her eyes crinkled. 'Bid them sew a fine gown for you to wear at my wedding. You will be coming to Garloch with Sir Ruari when I marry Sir Donald Gordon.'

Innes sat silent. Would Sir Ruari take her to Jane's wedding? Her heart stirred a little with excitement, thinking how much she would enjoy such an event, and how much she would enjoy ordering a lovely gown of her own. It would take the place of the wedding gown she had not worn. Suddenly she felt ashamed of rejecting the lovely gown which Jane must have worked on for her benefit.

'I am sorry I did not wear your gown,' she said.

'In truth I liked you the more for refusing to wear other than your own plumes, even if your feathers were bedraggled,' said Jane.

'Why did you sew it for me?' Innes asked.

Jane pursed her lips, then smiled a little. 'You had refused Sir Alexander,' she said. 'Sir Ruari was determined that you would not refuse him and . . . well

. . . he is a very determined man. You will not find marriage easy, Lady Innes. I look forward to a more comfortable life with Sir Donald.'

'Lady Margaret Gordon served the Queen at Edinburgh,' Innes began.

'Aunt to Sir Donald,' said Jane, breaking her thread.

'Then she will know that I am here at Glenallyn. Will it not make trouble for Sir Ruari?'

'He is not a man to hide from trouble. He will confound his enemies, and, if he can, make peace with them. He will grow powerful and will lead by his strength, and not confront . . . except for his greatest enemy . . . But you need have no fears, Lady Innes.'

'I wish you were not leaving,' Innes repeated, and Jane took her hand.

'I will be a friend to you,' she said, gently.

'But your sister . . . '

'Her life has crossed with yours,' said Jane. 'Wait a little until she is happy again. Just be happy that Sir Ruari loves you.'

Innes smiled rather grimly, thinking that Jane did not know Sir Ruari as well as she believed! She stood up as Lady Mary walked into the room, clad in her travelling cloak, acknowledging Innes with a slight bow.

'Sir Ruari is assembling his men,' she said, briskly. 'You must leave your mending, Jane, until we return to our home.'

'I hope you do not leave Glenallyn on my account, ma'am,' said Innes, awkwardly. 'I am sorry that your affairs have not turned out well for you.'

'It seems that you are fated to have what I cannot,' said Lady Mary, and it seemed to Innes that the shadow of Ruari stood between them. Why would she not have him? wondered Innes. Could it be that she had lost the child too easily?

'Sir Ruari sent a servant to find you, Lady Innes. He will wish to have a word with you before he leaves.'

'I had better go to him,' said Innes, and hurried along the cold grey stone corridor.

Ruari was in the great hall, but he scarcely looked at Innes when she arrived. Servants were hurrying here and there, and Matthew Drummond, squire to Sir Ruari, was being given last minute instructions for guarding Glenallyn.

'I leave the Lady Innes in your care, Matthew,' he said, 'and you, ma'am, will remain here until I return. I go on essential business, but I do not fear any skirmish which cannot be dealt with. Will Munro will escort you should you wish to wander around the precincts of the castle. Ah . . . the ladies are ready to leave . . . '

He turned again to Innes after Lady Mary and Mistress Jane had taken leave of her, then bent and kissed her swiftly.

'Whatever happens you are my wife and the mistress of Glenallyn,' he told her. 'Remember that. And ask your maid to burn that gown when you have another,' he said, his lip curling. 'Glenallyn is not Invernairn and even Invernairn is no longer a beggar stronghold. I did not marry a beggar maid!'

He was gone in a moment, and Innes stood where she was, for a long time, until the echo of horses' hooves had long since gone. The servants had eyed her surreptitiously for a moment as they went quietly about their duties, then noise gradually broke out.

Squire Matthew came over to talk to her. 'Is there anything you wish, ma'am?' he asked. 'If . . . if you have any trouble with the servant wenches now that the master has ridden out . . . '

'What? Oh . . . Squire Matthew . . . ' She had been deep in thought. Now she saw that the servants were running about, having eaten up the remnants of the food and wine, and were making no further attempt to clean up the great hall which still bore some marks of the revelry from the wedding feast. Perhaps they felt that the master had not lingered very long with his bride! she thought resentfully.

Innes remembered how well the place had been run in Sir Alexander's time, and suddenly she felt as though she were back in Dundallon, and helping the Lady Eleanor to look after the place after Sir Archibald had ridden out. She clapped her hands loudly, then lifted a large handbell from a shelf near the huge fireplace. This she banged so that the servants looked at her, startled, and others began to gather and stand to attention.

'There is a new mistress in Glenallyn,' she said, clearly. 'You will not find me a shrew . . . unless you do not carry out your duties to the best of your ability. I will see each one of you and learn what duties have been allocated to you. If they please me, you may carry on as before. If they do not, we will find others more suitable.

'Now, I want to see the great hall looking clean and sweet smelling with fresh rushes. Do not leave the cleaning to the dogs. I want to see that the well is not polluted, and that the courtyard is swept of dung instead of relying on the rain. I will see that the kitchens are clean and cooking pots made fresh, and linen washed. I will examine every apartment and see that they are fresh for guests. Squire Matthew will help me, but I will be pleased with those who are diligent and . . . and box the ears of the lazy. I do not mind the sound of laughter and song so long as it accompanies hard work. If you are troubled, I will listen and help if I can, but I will not listen to complaints, one against the other, unless they are justified.'

They began to move away slowly, then more swiftly, but there was no song as they set about their duties. Innes went up to the small room used by the ladies each morning, having set the sempstress to sew garments for her. The servants and retainers would have to get used to her, she thought with a sigh, but she would not have them lazy and idle, nor would she deal with them unfairly. Meg had taught her that. But if Glenallyn was well run, then even the servants would be happy.

11

Innes' new gowns were simple and practical, and she ordered the sewing women to make more handsome robes for her to wear when Sir Ruari returned. For the first few days she was busy and active, having Squire Matthew conduct her round Glenallyn and out into the courtyard, where she inspected the chambers within the castle curtain. It was finer than Dundallon, but Innes had grown used to Edinburgh which was even finer than Glenallyn.

She thought a great deal about Meg Bell, and asked Will Munro if he would ride to Leyburn with a message. She would make a hamper of some food and put in the gold coins Ruari had given her . . . which she had earned, thought Innes . . . and Meg would be comfortable and able to feed her family for many weeks.

But Will looked doubtful when she sent for him. 'The master bade me guard you, my Lady,' he told her. 'I cannot ride out and leave you here.'

'Is there anyone else I can send, Will?' she asked.

They regarded one another, each reading the other's mind. Sometimes henchmen were sent out on errands of mercy, with food and coins, and returned empty-handed swearing they had been set upon by robbers, but their own families had suddenly sported new shawls and bonnets.

'No one I can recommend, my Lady,' said Will, shaking his head. 'The maister can send out a party when he returns.'

But would the master do this for her? Innes wondered. She remembered the look on his face as he placed the coins into her hand. How could she know what black thoughts he was harbouring? And what would he say if she asked him to send a party of henchmen with these same coins for Meg Munro?

'I cannot ask the master, Will,' she said, sighing. 'It is not important to him. No, if you must look after me, then I will take the coins and the food and you will ride with me. We will ride with the same number of men who brought me here.'

'But, my Lady, I dare not!' cried Will. 'The orders were that you stay within the castle.'

'But Sir Ruari does not anticipate trouble or he would not have ridden out.'

'No, ma'am, but . . . ' Will looked unhappy. He had seen a mulish look descend on Innes' face and he recognised it. The young mistress was as fond of her own way as was the master. He was about to be caught between the two of them.

'I durst not go, my Lady,' he pleaded.

'Then Squire Matthew will go.'

'But Squire Matthew cannot leave Glenallyn.'

'Then I will go alone,' said Innes, flags of colour in her cheeks, 'since the men Sir Ruari has left to guard me appear to be no men at all. I am told that all is at peace, yet none dare venture out. The packmen are calling regularly; there are travellers abroad, and Leyburn is not a day's ride away ... hardly half a day. If we leave at dawn we can ride there and return in one day.'

'Nay, mistress, it grows dark too early.'

'Then we sleep at Leyburn. The men can rest in the barn if they are not too soft.'

Will flushed. 'I can pick fine strong men,' he told her. 'None are used to soft living.'

'We leave in the morning, Will. Meg was kind to me, and I do not forget my friends. She needs help. Thomas Bell is ill-tempered when there is not enough to feed their bellies. I want to help Meg.'

'I will take it, my lady,' said Will, 'even if the maister is also ill-tempered with me for disobeying orders.'

'No, Will, I will take it,' said Innes, firmly. 'It will be as I say.'

'Aye, ma'am,' said Will with a touch of relief. He was used to taking orders, not giving them.

Squire Matthew Drummond was very young and was earning his spurs in the service of Sir Ruari. Now, however, he felt worried and uncertain when he saw that Lady Innes was determined to ride out for two days, with Will Munro and a party of horsemen. Annie Hall would accompany her mistress.

'It is not seemly,' said Matthew.

'Why not, sir?' asked Innes. 'Must I be a prisoner in Glenallyn?'

'No, my Lady, but Sir Ruari . . . '

'Is not here, and I have business which requires my attention. Are you afraid that I shall run away, Squire Matthew? I assure you that Glenallyn is now my home, and I will be back before nightfall on the morrow. We stay for one night at Leyburn. Sir Ruari will remain in Edinburgh for three more days, and I shall be back before he returns.'

'I am uneasy, ma'am,' said Matthew, his young face flushed and rosy, so that he looked little more than a boy.

'You must guard Glenallyn well,' Innes told him, 'and see that my orders are carried out. Already Glenallyn looks better. We must have it fresh for Sir Ruari's return.'

'Aye, ma'am,' Matthew agreed, rather more eagerly now that he, too, had duties to carry out.

Innes, with Annie Hall, Will Munro and their party of horsemen, set out for Leyburn early the following morning. It was twilight when they reached Leyburn and there were signs that labourers had been working in the fields. A new door was being built on to the old farmstead and the roof being repaired. Innes reined in, looking at Will with a puzzled frown. It was only a short time since they had left the place which had been falling apart from sheer poverty, and now there were signs of new wealth such as Thomas Bell had not possessed.

Meg came to the door, still clad in her own gown, but her face paled when she saw Innes.

'It . . . it's yourself, Mistress,' she said. 'Ye have come back. Well, there is no shelter for you at Leyburn.'

'It would seem that Leyburn is in fine fettle,' said Innes. 'Where has your good fortune come from, Meg? Can it be that Thomas Bell has informed on me?'

'Oh no, Mistress Innes, never fear!' cried Meg, and Innes could not doubt the sincerity in her tone.

'It grows darker and we are tired, Meg,' she said. 'I have come to talk business with you.'

Meg gasped. 'You canna come in,' she cried, and Will stepped forward grimly.

'This is Lady Innes Stewart, wife to Sir Ruari Stewart,' he said, sternly. 'She needs shelter and would seek it in your home. She has her own servant to attend to her.'

'Lady Innes,' said Meg. 'Oh, my Lady . . . '

'Where is Thomas Bell?' Innes asked, and Meg stood aside reluctantly and allowed them into the farmstead.

'He has ridden to town for . . . for purchases,' said Meg.

'Ridden!'

'Aye we have bought a nag.'

'You have bought more than a nag,' said Innes. 'Somewhere there is a packman who is pouring blessings on you at this present time; but I see you are already well fed, even though I have brought provisions.'

'They will be welcome, my Lady,' cried Meg eagerly, 'very welcome.'

Innes was looking round. The children had crawled to their beds, but they had eaten well and the dogs devoured the scraps.

'Where is Janet?' she asked. 'You have moved her box.'

Meg began to sob. 'She is dead,' she whispered. 'She died the day you left, Mistress . . . my Lady . . . she rests in the churchyard.'

'Poor Janet . . . Oh, poor Janet . . . '

'Thomas sold her belongings; the treasures she kept in her box. We are spending money on Leyburn now.'

'On ribbons and fripperies,' said Innes, picking them up.

'On labour,' flashed Meg. 'On improvement for the farm. We buy an ox and a cart . . . '

'On Janet's treasures?' Innes picked up a long gold necklace which had belonged to Lady Eleanor. 'So Thomas Bell took the strongbox, Meg?'

Meg shook her head wildly. 'Nay, Lady Innes. It is my mother's treasure. She hid it in her box under the silks and satins and would let no one near. We found it when she died.'

'Was she bedridden from the first, Meg?'

'No, my Lady. She helped Thomas in the fields, then she took to wandering. Then her bones grew stiff and she could not move.'

'She must have gone for the strongbox and brought it here. How much is left, Meg?'

Meg produced the remnants of the jewels, and Innes held the jewelled ornaments in her hands.

'Do you mean to take them, my Lady?' asked Meg, half fearfully. 'Thomas will strike me dead most like.'

'They belong to the Frazers,' said Innes, 'but I have come with money and will buy them from you.'

'They do not deserve it, my Lady,' cried Will who had been looking on. 'They should be accused of thievery and brought to trial.'

'They gave me shelter when I had none,' said Innes. 'They shall have the gold, but I keep Lady Eleanor's jewels. I would have them for myself.'

Thomas Bell was glad to exchange the gems for gold when he arrived home, swaying a little from supping ale. He scowled at Innes, but she soon made it known that Meg must be left alone.

'Do ye seek shelter here?' he asked.

'Only for this night,' said Innes. 'We return to Glenallyn in the morning. I

299

came to provide for you.'

Thomas turned away. 'We only took what we thought was our own,' he muttered.

'You must have recognised the strongbox for which we searched together, Thomas Bell,' said Innes.

'He should be accused, ma'am,' put in Will.

'I have what is left, and they have gold enough,' said Innes. 'My debt is paid.'

★　★　★

There was a heavy mist over the countryside when Innes, with Annie Hall and the rest of the party prepared to leave for Glenallyn the following morning. Meg had gradually regained her good spirits when she realised that she would not lose the precious luxuries such as she had never believed would be hers. She could hardly believe that the jewelled trinkets which would have been sold so cheaply, had now been exchanged for more gold; and she thought about the gowns she could now buy, and the ornaments to brighten her home. The packmen would no longer pass Leyburn by.

Innes listened to her plans and shook her head. Meg and Thomas Bell had little idea how to use extra money. They might prosper the farm a little, but they would spend any money gained, and would soon be poor again. She spared a tear for poor Janet, who had lost her mind and who had tried to protect her riches; but they had been kept for Lady Eleanor, not Innes.

The corner of the room was now empty, and Janet was at rest.

Thomas Bell had gone out early, having avoided Innes as much as he could. He had grown quiet and rather sullen, after she refused to accuse him of taking the contents of her strongbox, but said he must have known its true owner. As they were about to ride off, Thomas suddenly appeared from the barn.

'Lady Innes!' he called, and she paused for a moment.

'Aye, Thomas.'

'Ye have been good to me and mine,' he said, awkwardly. 'My thanks, ma'am. Mind out for the soldiers. They were riding to the north yesterday.'

Innes nodded, then smiled. 'We will be careful. God be with you and yours, Thomas Bell.'

The mist thickened as they rode up into higher ground, and there was a faint glow of red from the eastern sky. Innes' clothing felt damp and chilled, but her heart was more at peace. She would have to ask Ruari to forgive her for accusing him of taking her strongbox. She must have been mad to be so certain that he was to blame, and to accuse him without any real proof. But she had felt humiliated by her lack of wordly goods when he practically forced marriage on to her. She had wanted to be a bride who had her own competence, and not a beggar maid.

'Best hurry, my Lady,' said Will, uneasily as they neared Glenallyn. 'We are nearly into the gloaming, and I would feel pleased to be over the drawbridge before nightfall. I have a lack of ease in me.'

Innes, too, had been experiencing a strange lack of ease as they rode into the shadows, and as they neared the precincts of Glenallyn, there seemed to be a great many shadows. Then, suddenly, Innes' heart leapt into her mouth as the land seemed to be thundering with soldiers, and blood-curdling cries rent the air. She saw Will and the other men turn to fight, and one of her own henchmen being cut down even as Will thrust her behind him, and men from Glenallyn thundered into the fray.

Innes heard the clank of swords and the cries of injured men mingling with the frightened screams of the horses, and saw the burning vegetation as parts of Glenallyn were put to the torch.

Suddenly she was seized as Will was knocked to the ground, and she screamed with terror as a light from a burning haystack revealed a face close to her own. It was a face out of her nightmares — the scarred leering face of James Livingstone.

'So I have captured you at last, Mistress Frazer,' he cried. 'You will not find it so easy to burn me this time.'

They were close to a wooded area, and he threw her to the ground, pinning her with his great strength so that she could not move. She was too frightened to scream, and could only make croaking sounds in her throat as the weight of his arm forced her head down. Her damp cloak had wrapped itself tightly round her body and she could hear his muttered curses as he tried to tear the thick garment from her, even as she struggled wildly.

The sounds of fighting had multiplied so that the noise of battle was a great roar in her head, and she vaguely realised that many more men had joined in the skirmish. They had no chance, thought Innes. James Livingstone would have his way with her; then she would be thrown to the soldiers until she was dead, like Eleanor.

She tried to bite him, but he seemed to be enjoying her helplessness, and gradually she felt her clothing being ripped apart. She thought about poor Will who had looked after her so faithfully, and she thought about Ruari . . . Ruari!

She managed to pull her head aside and screamed his name, even though it seemed that no sound came. But even as she began to feel pain in her lower parts, there was a rush of warmth pouring on to her shoulder and the enormous weight of James Livingstone crushed on top of her body.

Horrified, Innes saw that her body was soaked in blood; then the weight of the dead man was pushed from her and she was lifted up.

'My poor dove,' said Ruari. 'My poor

sweet wife. Thank God I was in time . . . '

'Oh . . . Ruari,' sobbed Innes, 'Ruari . . . '

Then she was being whirled into a great black void.

12

Innes lay in the great softly-feathered bed at Glenallyn, and wept for Annie Hall and two of the henchmen from their party. Sarah Laidlaw sponged her forehead with vinegar to reduce the fever, and offered her soothing syrups and nourishing drinks.

'I want nothing, Sarah,' Innes said, dully. 'I am responsible for Annie's death, and I have killed those men by taking them away from their duties.'

'They would have fought for ye here, ma'am,' said Sarah. 'It is only the fever which makes ye think this way. Annie was a friend o' mine, but she was always careless. She could have hid in the gloaming but she allowed herself to be caught.'

'I was caught, too,' said Innes.

'They were looking for ye, ma'am. There are spies everywhere. It is a great blessing that the maister returned when he did.'

Innes turned away. Ruari had not come to see her. She remembered his voice shouting out of the mist, then fading as she was swept down into darkness; but since she awoke, he had not come.

'Where is the master?' she asked.

'He is very busy, ma'am,' said Sarah, sponging her forehead again. 'After a battle such as was fought out there, there is much to do. Men were . . . were killed and others injured. Poor Will Munro is injured, but he will soon recover. The soldiers have been carried in for attention, and the women are putting healing herbs on the wounds. The others . . . ' Sarah's voice trailed off, but Innes said no more. The bodies would, perhaps, be plundered and then buried. It was the nature of things. At least Will had not lost his life and best of all, Ruari was safe.

Innes moved her aching arms and touched her own body. She shuddered and felt sick when she remembered James Livingstone, but at least he had not injured her. She was black and blue with bruises, but those would heal. But it was she who had brought this quarrel to Ruari, and her heart was sick at the thought.

'Drink this, Lady Innes,' Sarah commanded, and she drank the cooling liquid. Seconds later she was asleep again.

Ruari Stewart was sitting at Innes' bedside when she once again opened her eyes. It had grown dark but the firelight flickered on his dark face, and the candles made a halo of his crisp curling hair.

He turned to her as she stirred, and her eyes were wide and as dark as her hair as she stared up at him.

'I am sorry, Ruari,' she whispered. 'It was all my fault. I made Will take me to Leyburn with . . . with food and money for Meg. I . . . I thought they needed it, but . . . Ruari . . . please do not be angry with him.'

He bent over her. 'Are you afraid of me, Innes?'

Her eyes told their own story.

'God forgive me,' he said, stroking her hair. 'I . . . '

'You will not want me here,' she interrupted. 'I am no proper wife for you, Ruari. You can send me to the Queen.'

'The Queen no longer desires any vengeance,' Ruari said soothingly. 'Dundallon will be returned to you, if I succeed in helping Crichton. My only desire is to serve the new King, because only by owing allegiance to our rightful King do we hope to hold our country together. Otherwise we tear one another apart.'

'Livingstone wanted to be revenged on me,' Innes whispered, and Ruari's hold on her fingers almost crushed them.

'He was my only enemy,' said Ruari. 'He might have taken you, my dove, and I had murder in my heart.'

'But . . . but you cannot love me,

Ruari, as I love you,' she said. 'Why did you not marry Lady Mary?'

'Because I have loved you since I first saw you,' said Ruari. 'Because I wanted you and wanted you, but I had nothing to offer you, my dearest Innes. I was a beggar lord, trying to restore Invernairn and out of favour with the King. How could I keep you safe, you a Lady born, with only a handful of beggars to serve us? I knew it would take years of service to restore Invernairn. So I tried to marry you to my cousin, because I knew you would be safe and sheltered at Glenallyn, though my heart had to be hardened to do it. Then you would have none of it!'

'I did not love Alexander,' she cried. 'I loved you. I would have been a beggar for you.'

He bent and kissed her lingeringly.

'You were a wildcat. You insulted Alexander, and he gave you to the Queen as a nursemaid for her children. It appealed to his queer sense of humour. I thought he would take you to the Hamiltons, but he knew that the Queen would not seek vengeance when she began to know you and to love you. He did not know that Livingstone had raped Dundallon, and that you would recognise him in Edinburgh. He did not know that you were in danger from Livingstone, nor did I until it was too late.'

'He slew Eleanor as I watched,' said Innes, dully, 'and her babies.'

'He will do so no more,' said Ruari, stroking her hair. 'I knew he would seek you out in Invernairn and Glenallyn after Will brought you away.' Ruari was silent for a while, 'and for a long time I thought I had lost you. I was mad for you, but even my servants thought I was mad against you. No one told me where you were, and in my anxiety I forgot about Leyburn. When I knew you were there, I had Will bring you to me at once, and arranged our wedding straight away. I could not lose you again, my dove. And to think that that brute almost destroyed you.'

Innes lay still. Gradually it was beginning to dawn on her that Ruari loved her and cared for her.

'I accused you of taking the strong-box, but now I have Eleanor's jewellery,' she said. 'Janet was looking after it at Leyburn, yet I accused you . . . can you forgive me, Ruari?'

'We hurt one another,' he said, rather sadly. 'It is always the way when a man and a woman love one another as we do, but our happiness will far out-weigh our miseries. We will have great happiness here at Glenallyn, if we love one another, and serve our King.'

'I will go anywhere and do anything so long as you love me, Ruari,' she said, softly.

He lifted her tenderly from the bed and held her in his arms, then kissed her passionately.

'Do you blame me for rushing you to the priest?' he asked.

'Even when I looked like a beggar maid?'

'You looked like a Queen,' he told

her, against her ear. 'Innes Stewart of Glenallyn, are you all mine?'

'All yours, Ruari,' she agreed, and he went to close and lock the door.

THE END